The Conversions

Also by Harry Mathews

The Sinking of the Odradek Stadium
Tlooth

The Conversions

HARRY MATHEWS

CARCANET

Published in Great Britain 1988 by
Carcanet Press Limited
208–212 Corn Exchange Buildings
Manchester M4 3BQ

Published in the USA 1987 by
Carcanet
198 Sixth Avenue
New York, NY 10013

British Library Cataloguing in Publication Data

Mathews, Harry
The conversions.
I. Title
813′.54[F]   PS3563.A8359

ISBN 0-85635-766-9

The publisher acknowledges the financial
assistance of the Arts Council of Great Britain

Printed in England by SRP Ltd, Exeter

The Conversions

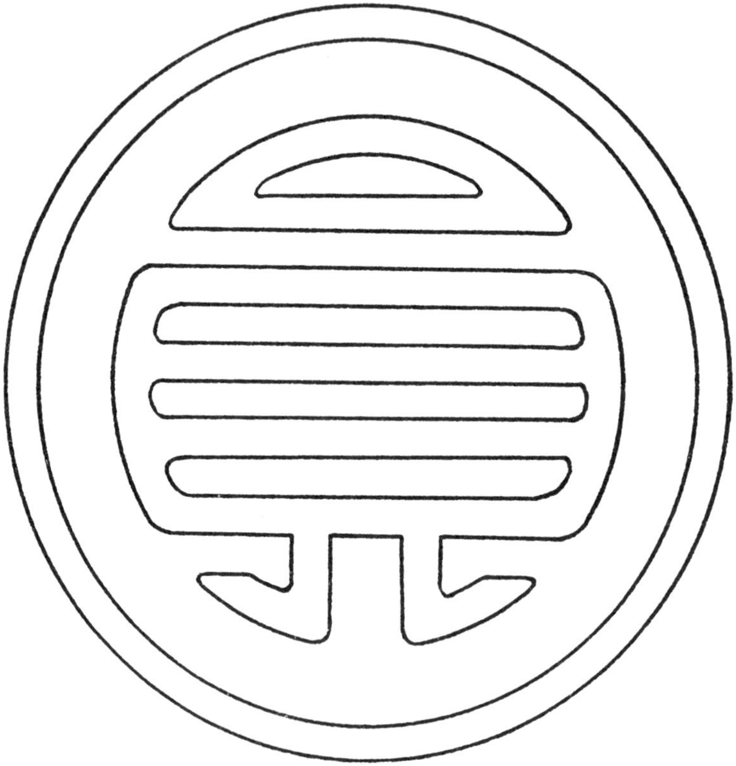

•

THE ADZE

The wealthy amateur Grent Wayl invited me to his New York house for an evening's diversion. Welcoming me, he said: The cheek of our Bea! pointing to his niece, Miss Beatrice Fod, who, accompanied on the harmonium by her brother Isidore, sang to assembled guests.

At night when you're asleep
  Without no pants on
Into your tent I'll creep
  Without no pants on

Such nervous speech! Why should he mind, since the song delighted the company? Mr. Wayl was aging, aging; but no one would take his words lightly.

He led me upstairs to see one of his new acquisitions. In the library Mr. Wayl laid an oblong case of green leather on a white table. Having turned on a ceiling spotlight to illuminate the case, he opened it. A weapon rested on the brilliant red lining, its smooth handle of ash, its billshaped flat blade of gold.

According to Mr. Wayl, the instrument was a ritual adze. The side of the bill we had first beheld was plain, but its reverse was chased with wiry engravings, depicting seven scenes. Six had in common the figure of a longhaired woman with full breasts and a face crosshatched for swarthiness. Mr. Wayl suggested that the woman was some heroine or saint, and that the engravings told her life. He looked at me curiously while he said this.

Mr. Wayl asked me to interpret the series of engravings.

I began with the leftmost scene, in the point of the blade, where the woman stood naked at the mouth of a stream, with a pile of cowrie shells at her feet. The subject hardly suited the life of a saint, but I took it to be a decorative conceit—a quaint medieval mixture of pagan and Christian themes.

To the right of this, the woman stood upon clouds, above a throng of striped men bearing staves shaped like inverted L's. Below the clouds a disc emanated crooked spikes, while lower still people on the earth raised their hands. This clearly seemed to be the saint's manifestation, a descent from heaven. The stave-bearing figures were angels with pennons, the spiked disc the rejoicing sun.

In the next engraving the woman held one side of a small wreath; a man in simple vestments held the opposite side. I thought this man must be Christ presenting the saint with a crown of holiness.

The fourth scene showed the woman among battling knights, who were drawn gruesome and pathetic. The saint was surely putting an end to some battle, if not to war itself.

Next, the woman appeared outside a burning grove. Within it there were many tormented figures. She lifted her arms in supplication, as would befit one pleading for the damned.

In the sixth scene the woman knelt in front of a mitred priest who stretched his left hand over her. A fire, which I interpreted as a symbol of divine love, burned in the background. I had no doubt the scene showed the saint blessed by some pope.

The woman did not figure in the last engraving. I supposed it to be decorative, like the first one: radii of one small arc, four arrows pointed to symbols representing the quarters of the moon. A bag of fish—possibly a Christian reference—hung below.

Mr. Wayl had grown impatient during my remarks. He now exclaimed: You're as dumb as is!

Excuse me, sir, I said, if your pleasure was marred.

He was suddenly friendly: No one with purple eyes is stupid. But do you have perfect pitch?

I answered that I had. Leaving the library, he took the adze with him.

•

PREPARATIONS

As we descended the stairs Mr. Wayl stopped me. Listen! Miss Fod was singing:

> The second queen was an Amazon
> With a terrible spear of brass

Such music! said Mr. Wayl. A real old tune—a lass's tenor. You must recognize it.

I listened:

> Whistling the devil's salvation
> In a girdle of crimson cowries

The three queens made thunder
And snapped stones with a feather
But Black Jack was the smartest crack
And married them all together

There was applause. Mr. Wayl had left me listening; he now stood, encircled by the company, next to his niece and nephew. Following his summons I joined them.

Tonight's game, he said, will be a race. The contestants are Bea and Is, whom you all know, and—his hand on my shoulder—this gentleman. The prize will be my antique adze.

Servants entered to draw back the curtains at one side of the drawing-room, then to open the sliding panels of glass that formed the wall behind. We overlooked a greenhouse, whose fragrant heat rose quickly about us, but which we could see little of: it was unlighted except for three parallel bands, about two yards long, that were sunk in its floor near us. These shone dull green.

That is the course, said Mr. Wayl. The bands, which are covered with a thin layer of salt slime, are lighted from below so that you can follow the race.

The contestants will be represented by these. He held out his opened cigarette case: in it lay small sticks of tobacco-colored stuff with a tuft of tangled white thread at the end of each.

Worms called zephyrs. They are dried out but alive; moisture will quicken them. On the course, which is wet, they will find in front of them a trail of their habitual food (tiny pharaohs) that will lead them to the finish.

As for the human contestants, they will do more than watch. Each must accompany his worm's advance with an ascending major scale, to be played on one of these instruments; as you doubtless know, they are named serpents.

Mr. Wayl detached three S-ish wooden tubes from a wall panel behind him, fitted their lesser ends with silver mouthpieces, and silently demonstrated a scale on one of them, progressively unstopping its six finger-holes. The lowest and highest notes were obtained with all the holes stopped.

It is curious, he said, that the holes are divided into groups of three by a length of wood having no proportion to the acoustical distance between the fourth and fifth notes of the scale. Nor do the spaces between the other holes vary with the interval; the holes are apparently bored for the convenience of the fingers. Yet the results are just. Thus with all holes open: see? With one: *re*. With three: *fa*. (Since these are C-serpents, the scale names are true.)

At the beginning of the race each contestant will play the lower *do*. The course bands are marked with six indentations; as his worm passes them the contestant must sound the subsequent tones—*re* at the first marker, *mi* at the second, and so on. Without this accompaniment the worm's progress counts for nothing. The race will end with the first high *do*.

Mr. Wayl gave us our instruments.

For you, Bea, a fine French example made for the Duchess of Lissixg, who was known as "the Imp Queen"—but I can't remember the Latin for imp.

Is will have the favorite serpent of Dericar Ciorc, the virtuoso.

And you will have this one. It's wound with masking tape to cover some disturbing scenes painted on it; otherwise it's sound.

Take your places.

We entered the conservatory and knelt, each with a horn, at the end of our appointed bands. Servants knelt next to us, ready with our quiet worms.

Presently the drawing-room lights went out. Mr. Wayl said, Begin.

THE RACE

Do: unevenly, the three horns gave the note in the near darkness. The servants placed our worms in the reviving ooze. I watched mine through the green-lighted fringe of the foxtail mat on which I knelt: it lay still. To my left Beatrice Fod urged hers on with whispers, then blew a new note on her serpent—a hesitant semitone.

Patience, said Mr. Wayl from the threshold of the drawing-room.

There was a faint white light in the greenhouse, barely more than a drifting phosphorescence. My worm curled, untangling the bunched thread at his tip in thin exploratory tentacles that looked like rapid-flowering vine tendrils. His tan body was now a pale whitish-green. Moving, he glided quick over the green glass in a curious curve. My eyes were already numb from straining in the dim light when he swerved around the first black marker.

Re I sounded clearly; but Beatrice followed only with her faltering C-sharp. There was laughter from the next room. Turning I saw its cause: an old guest sitting in an overstuffed chair nodded drowsily among the onlookers. Some sort of dark-blue light had been made to shine on him, and against the faint phosphorescent whiteness that still filled the air he appeared to be covered with thick soot. Despite the laughter, he dozed on.

My zephyr slid swiftly forward. It was then I noticed that the path he had taken was marked by a nearly invisible trail of black: a broken irregular line.

Beatrice, in spite of her worm's advance, could not force her intermittent C-sharp to the desired *re.* Is Fod as yet made no sound. My worm touched the second marker. I played

Mi, followed by a sigh of wonder from the watchers, while under my eyes the worm's black trail suddenly turned a sullen green. Looking up, I saw on the wall beyond the course's finish the prize adze, flashing red in some beam cast on it from an unseen point. The vision was the color of my inner eye! I nearly forgot to follow my worm; and when I next observed him he was already at the third marker.

Fa: my lips and lungs blared the note out while my eyes fixed the fiery adze: but as I played, it dropped abruptly into darkness. Again there was a bustle in the drawing-room. All now looked towards the glass case, placed on a small stand in the center of the room, where the fifteen-pound Slauss sapphire was exposed. The jewel glowed as if illuminated from within: its clarity was now clustered with entwined tenuous red veins. We beheld it thus for a few moments until we heard an unexpected *re* from Is Fod's serpent. As soon as the note was sounded the sapphire turned a translucent black that darkened but did not obscure the red skein within.

When my zephyr attained the fourth marker, I made my only mistake of the race. With *fa* I had unstopped the last of the first set of fingerholes. Between it and the next hole lay the abnormal extent of closed tube that Mr. Wayl had mentioned. Uncovering the *sol* hole I tried to compensate for its position by slackening my lips; I only succeeded in producing a faltering *fa diesis.*

Every light was extinguished, even the faint green course-lights. An unusual darkness suffused the conservatory and the drawing-room. Without color or light, it seemed to have its own thick splendor; and this impression was confirmed when I found that I could still barely discern the line trailed by the advancing worm. I recognized too that this line formed not a haphazard figure, but letters.

I had forgotten to correct my mistake. Only when the silence that followed the sudden darkness had been broken by the embarrassed coughing of Miss Dryrein (Mr. Wayl's secretary) did I remember to play.

Sol: the chocolate blackness was at once pierced by a moving ray of yellow light.

I call this Midas's finger, said Mr. Wayl. And in fact whatever the beam touched acquired the luster and massiveness of gold. The sapphire, the harmonium, Mr. Wayl, Miss Dryrein, and, one by one, all the guests were subjected to the illusory transformation. Ima Mutés, the Catalan *entreteneuse*, was applauded: her evening gown was made of a tightly coiled spiral of velvet snakes.

The yellow beam was entering the greenhouse when Is Fod sounded his *mi*. The adze again turned a brilliant red. When the yellow ray came to rest on it, its red did not change to gold but deepened in the midst of a golden haze.

The light had proved me right: my worm had left letters in his trail—in the reflected yellow they glowed purple. But I had no time to study them. My worm was at the fifth marker.

La. The adze again disappeared, as well as the moving beam. Instead violet light flooded that drowsy guest whom we had last seen covered with soot. This time the laughter of the other guests roused him, and he opened his eyes, which flashed weirdly, casting thin lilac-colored shafts into the surrounding darkness. A girl cried out, *O Papa, tu m'fais peur!* The old man went back to sleep. The worm-letters took on yellowness, while the course was black in the violet glow.

Beatrice uttered a final breath into her serpent: still the same quavering C-sharp, dull whiteness guttering for a moment about the violet guest. Balls! We heard a whirring noise and a brief splintering of glass as Beatrice skied her horn through the conservatory roof. Draughts of February air swirled about us.

My *si* was followed at once by Is Fod's *fa*. Pink

flooded the course, its bands turning blue, the leech's trail a brighter yellow. At the end of each band a pool of purple light revealed our worms' goal: spider crabs, with ponderous claws and backs overgrown with trailing parasites. Opposite me the crab, seeing his prey so close, waited, while the one facing Is Fod started at a sluggish pace after his. Beatrice's worm had already been eaten.

I watched the eyestalks of the waiting crab lower. Just as the nippers pinched the slender swerving body Mr. Wayl said to me, Finish. The high *do* came satisfactorily forth, the air was filled for a moment with a kind of swimming silver, and finally in greenhouse and drawing-room the lights went on. My eyes were tired and blurred. When they cleared, the course bands were empty of light, leeches, and crabs. There only remained the trail of triturated food and slime my lost worm had left, broken marks of a shiny blackness among which I recognized certain letters:

e as no s ex rex noth Syl i

Get rid of that, Mr. Wayl said to a servant. To me: That was not what I meant. I tried to lay down his food so that he would spell . . . But the result is nothing—fragments.

The race had lasted an hour. Taking my prize with me, I soon left.

FIRST INQUIRIES

I found out why Mr. Wayl thought my eyes were purple: he was colorblind. Other remarks of his remained obscure—why, for instance, had he felt that I should recognize the song Beatrice had been singing when we left the library? Throughout the evening Mr. Wayl had treated me with singular attention. He had shown me the adze privately. From a large company of guests he had chosen me to compete with the two Fods, known to be his only heirs. He had been pleased, and not at all surprised, that I won the contest. Why?

As Mr. Wayl had taken pains to interest me in the images worked on the face of the adze-head, I thought it might be rewarding to learn more about them. So a few days after the party I called Miss Dryrein to ask her for any information she had concerning the adze. While she knew next to nothing herself (Mr. Wayl had secreted, in a safety-box to which she had no access, what relevant documents there were), she suggested I consult the former owner of the adze, from whom it had been bought only a few months before.

This person, a minor novelist, at once agreed to see me. I called at his apartment in Bethune Street one evening and there, with a bottle of pisco to maintain us, he told me what he knew.

"THE SORES"

It was on a night in the autumn of last year that I came into possession of the adze. Late one afternoon I had gone to the Plaza, where a cocktail party was being given in connection with the publication of one of my books. Perhaps you've read it—a short novel called *The Sores*? It was dark when I left. I was in an impressionable state; I had drunk a lot, and eaten little, and the hours of party talk had left me agitated. I remember standing on the steps of the hotel when I left, suddenly exalted by the cold air and the illuminated city. A sweet restlessness came over me. I decided to hire one of the carriages drawn up on the Park side of Fifty-ninth Street for a long drive. At first I could not find a willing driver, but one at last agreed to take me out to a Long Island beach. He warned me the trip would last through the night; but I had no objection to that.

We set off, soon crossing the Queensborough Bridge. I'm not sure where we went afterwards—I think we started out through Maspeth and later skirted South Ozone. I don't know the city well at all, and in any case I was soon sunk in my dreams. I thought about my childhood, women, and the war, I recited poems and sang through scenes of opera, I thought of the future, especially of trips I would like to make to Morocco, to Sweden, to Afghanistan. Later I thought of the evening I had just passed, and finally of my book. I hadn't really thought of the book in a long time, having been too busy proofing it and discussing it with readers, publishers and reviewers. Softly shaken in the slow carriage, I renewed my lost enthusiasm.

It concerns three American men who meet in the restaurant of the Copenhagen airport. Their acquaintance begins at the smörgåsbord table, where each reveals a taste for bitter pickled onions. All three are waiting for the same flight, a departure for San Francisco across the Arctic Sea. At first they would seem to have nothing more in common. One of them, Jacob Pendastrava, is a sociologist, recently engaged on an inquiry into the variables of joy. Pownoll Toker Williaus is vice-president of a company that manufactures foundation garments, the Press-You-Nigh Stays, Inc. Noah La Vas, the youngest of the three, is an engineer whose specialty is the slowing of high winds. He has recently invented a kind of inverted pendulum which, projected into a wind-channel by powerful hydraulic springs, tends to set up restraining crosscurrents.

Their first conversation lags. Williaus hums nervously to fill the silence. La Vas in surprise recognizes the tune: Why that's *Wehe Wintgen Wehe*! What! says Williaus, You mean . . . This is too good to be true, adds Pendastrava. They have found a common enthusiasm; they are all three amateurs of old German music. A jubilant discussion of Sweelinck, Schein and Schütz, illustrated with musical examples, lasts until boarding time and through the first hours of flight.

When fatigue overcomes the majority of the passengers (very late in the night, for since it is June the plane is flying in sunlight), the three men, respecting the sleep of their fellow travelers, withdraw to the lounge in the tail of the plane. They too are tired, and they decide to play cards for a while. Pendastrava teaches his friends an antique form of cribbage. They have played for about an hour, and Williaus has just completed his fifteen with a jack of spades, when the cards and markers suddenly swarm in the air around them. Then they themselves are pitched from their chairs as the plane falls. The crash occurs; they find themselves battered but alive. La Vas succeeds in getting outside. He finds that the tail-section of the plane, broken off from the bulk of the fuselage, is resting on a flat expanse of ice. Before him there is a huge hole of black water. There is no sign of any other survivor or wreckage.

Williaus joins La Vas, and the two of them help Pendastrava, whose left leg is broken, down on to the ice. Making him as comfortable as possible, they return to the wreck to see what they can salvage. They find several pieces of handluggage, a considerable quantity of clothing, and some blankets. The luggage in the hold and the stores in the galley are lost. The two men search the handluggage diligently for food: all they find is a half-dozen cans and pots of dainties, souvenirs of tourists homeward bound: pâté de foie gras, smoked eel, sweetbreads in wine, pickled mushrooms, an Edam cheese, and a bottle of *grappa*. From the remaining contents of the luggage, La Vas and Williaus take several tubes of aspirin, a sheath knife, a compass, and a pistol (a small .30-caliber automatic) with two boxes of cartridges.

The next concern of the two men is Pendastrava's leg. La Vas proves his ingenuity by disassembling and reshaping the metal tubes out of which the lounge furniture is made. From them, with the aid of belts and wire, he constructs a huge splint. Shaped like a U with one side greater than the other, this splint, fitted into the groin and armpit of the injured man, not only keeps his leg rigid but also serves as a fixed crutch, enabling him to stand without having his leg touch the ground or support his body's weight.

Everything to be taken from the plane is brought out, for the wrecked tail is slowly sinking through the ice. The three men consider their situation. They decide that since a search will surely be made to discover the fate of their plane, they should stay next to the wreck, where they have a better chance of being seen from the air, until it sinks. On the other hand, they decide to prepare for the worst, that is, for a long trek southward over the ice in case they are not soon rescued. Thus the small amount of food at their disposal is to be severely rationed, and a part, the can of eel, set aside for use as fish-bait. Seawater is to be drunk from the start to avoid the harmful effects it might have if taken after prolonged thirst.

Most of the day has passed. Williaus spends the early evening preparing a tent out of blankets. La Vas fishes in the hole made by the sunken plane, but he has no luck. The morale of the men is good, tired as they are. Only Pendastrava shows any signs of despondency—his leg has been hurting him considerably. Even he becomes cheerful after a swallow of *grappa*. The three men sing *Ein fester Burg ist unser Gott*, in Schütz's harmonization. They feel no touch of loneliness in that lifeless tract of raw whiteness, but sleep well through the sunny night, La Vas and Williaus taking turns to watch.

The morning of the next day passes without event. The weather is bright and mild. La Vas explores the vicinity of their camp, finding nothing. Williaus fishes for several hours without success. Pendastrava rests; his leg bothers him less.

At midday a fire of sorts is made, and the can of sweetbreads is heated and half eaten.

During the afternoon an airplane, flying at about a thousand feet, passes many miles to the north of them. Of the several search planes sent out, this is the only one the survivors ever see.

The following day Pendastrava makes his first attempt to walk, but is obliged to give up after a few steps. His general condition has nonetheless improved.

On the afternoon of the fifth day the tail wreckage disappears. The hole it leaves is separated by only a few feet from the larger one caused by the crash; the two holes soon become one. The men decide to abandon their efforts to catch fish, preserving their bait for richer waters.

The next day, the sixth, the pot of goose-liver pâté is opened, the mushrooms, as well as the sweetbreads, having been finished. Pendastrava, who is exhausted by the few steps he has managed to take earlier in the day, vomits the small share of pâté he swallows. This causes the first break in morale since the crash: La Vas loses his temper and berates Pendastrava for his weakness and stupidity. Pendastrava answers feebly but bitterly.

In the course of the afternoon Williaus tries to reconcile his companions. He evidently succeeds. That night, however, at the hour when the three men usually sang together, Pendastrava refuses to join them. His excuse is that he cares too much for the music, which requires four voices, to like hearing it botched by three. But it is his silence that makes the singing impossible: La Vas and Williaus give up their sad duet. For the first time the three find the lifeless silence heavy, and the night sun sharp. All sleep little.

Matters do not improve next morning. A running argument begins between La Vas and the other men. La Vas insists that they start southward at once since a week has already passed and the efforts to find them have probably been abandoned: they must cover ground while they still have some food. The others feel that the departure must be postponed as long as possible so that Pendastrava's injured leg may heal—otherwise, how can they make any worthwhile progress?

The discussion is interminable and pointless. The

three men are starting to get weak, not so much from the lack of nourishment as from exposure. The glare of ice and sun is wrecking their eyes, and making them suffer from almost uninterrupted headaches. The consumption of seawater, minimal but constant, has also had its effect in the pain and cramp that molest their bowels. They are no longer reasonable and only La Vas has much energy for facing the problems of their predicament. The other two—especially Pendastrava—prefer to take refuge in a lethargic hope of rescue.

The senseless argument immobilizes the survivors. Scoring small points in the harangues becomes their main preoccupation, each man clinging to his point of view in spite of fact or need. La Vas is absurdly brutal during the first days of the argument, when Pendastrava's leg is in truth unfit for a day's march; while to safeguard the importance of his injury, the latter will not exercise his leg even when he feels capable of doing so. Williaus, in his role of nurse and protector, seconds this passivity.

It is not until six more days have passed that the three men break camp and start south. There is practically no more food: they have finished the eel, except for two slivers kept as bait, and nearly half the Edam cheese.

Nevertheless the departure is a boon for their spirits. Pendastrava is heroic in his efforts to advance, while the other two work in relay to help him and, during the rests, to take care of him. By evening they have advanced seven miles, according to La Vas's estimate. Although they are too tired to speak much, a new fellowship unites them.

The following day, the fifteenth after the crash,

Pendastrava's condition permits them to cover only about five miles. A long rest is salutary: a march of eight miles is made the next day, ten the day after that, and this average is kept up for two days more. The travelers observe a few seabirds, too distant to shoot at.

On the morning of the twentieth day, Pendastrava takes a hard fall on the ice. His leg hurts him terribly when he resumes his march. He is obliged to rest every two or three minutes and can advance only several hundred yards in an hour. The day's march is of less than three miles, only one mile having been covered after his fall.

Pendastrava is worse the next morning: his leg is swollen and sore. Even helped by his companions he is hardly able to walk at all, and the other men are far too weak to carry him. They barely advance a mile in nine hours. By that time the men are frantic with fatigue and despair. Pendastrava is in continual pain. He refuses to speak to the others.

During the night Pendastrava filches and eats the remaining morsel of cheese. His act is discovered at noon the next day, after five hours of painful meager progress. La Vas begins kicking the prostrate Pendastrava. When Williaus intervenes, La Vas knocks him down.

In the middle of the afternoon, during a prolonged rest, La Vas takes Williaus aside. He apologizes for having struck him, and goes on to give his view of their predicament: the only way out is to abandon Pendastrava. With him they will starve; without him, there is a chance that the two of them will reach the edge of the Arctic basin where they will find a plenty of fish and birds. Since it is inhuman to leave Pendastrava to die slowly, he should be shot. La Vas offers to do this, and asks Williaus to give him the pistol. Williaus refuses, wishing to think over the other's plan.

The march is resumed. When it is his turn to help Pendastrava, Williaus lets La Vas go a ways ahead of them. He then tells Pendastrava of La Vas's plan. Pendastrava demands the gun, and Williaus gives it to him. The sun is low, and a soft wind rises.

Williaus calls La Vas to take his turn with the injured man. Setting Pendastrava down on the ice, Williaus draws a few steps away, and stands turned away from the others. He hears La Vas cry out and looking around sees that Pendastrava is aiming the gun not at La Vas, but at him. La Vas runs slowly towards Pendastrava; Williaus screams; Pendastrava aims but holds his fire. When Pendastrava finally becomes aware of La Vas's approach, he turns the pistol towards him and shoots him through the chest. The stricken man falls on Pendastrava. Williaus's terror of Pendastrava changes to infinite anger and he runs whimpering to punish him. The latter is pinned beneath the dying La Vas and cannot even speak. Williaus strikes and scratches at his face. At last, seeing the gun lying on the ice where it has slid from Pendastrava's hand, he crawls to get it and returns to strike Pendastrava repeatedly in the face with the gun butt. Pendastrava struggles helplessly, trapped under La Vas's body. He is soon killed by the blows.

Shaking and exhausted, Williaus collapses on the ice near the two bodies. He lies there for almost three hours. He cannot find the strength to decide to get up. When he finally does, he leaves without looking at the others, keeping only his blankets and the pistol.

He does not rest until late that night. From now on he pays no more attention to the time of day, but walks when he can and rests when he must. He rests very often. He is now so weak that he cannot advance more than four or five miles a day. Since he has left the compass in La Vas's pocket, his progress south is even slower than this.

Twenty-five days have passed since the plane crash. Williaus talks to himself silently as he walks. He talks also (but silently still) to others. Curiously enough—he apologizes for his lapse—he cannot pronounce certain words, those that end in -ion. At first he can pronounce all their syllables except the last. Consternat, ambit—his groping tongue fails. Later he has difficulty pronouncing any part of such words. He tries pretending to think of other words and his mind then comes close to filling the hiatus. But when he springs towards the forgotten word there is only a ridiculous fragment—vat, sump—or a void.

He has seen birds more frequently, although only singly. He decides to start trying to shoot them. He notices that one of the birds seems to be following him—not only following but drawing closer with each succeeding hour. It is a rather large bird, of a sooty blue, which he recognizes as a noddy—the silly bird that is afraid of nothing. He cannot understand how this bird could have come so far north. He feels a strange hope seeing it.

When the bird is hovering about ten yards over his head, Williaus begins shooting at it. He misses repeatedly. The bird is not frightened and continues its daylong descent.

Williaus leaves off shooting at the bird when it is a

few feet from him. Not only are his shots useless, but the noddy appears to him like an angelic companion. The bird flies lower and lower, the undersides of its wings unnaturally white.

On the morning of the twenty-seventh day the white-sooty wings brush Williaus's face. He thinks: The foolish noddy, unafraid of man. The bird rises a little in the air only to cover his face again with its wings. He is snowblind.

Williaus does not at first understand what has happened to him. He walks through universal whiteness until he falls. After that he crawls for a while.

The noddy has not left him, but hovers in his unblinded mind. The bird darkens, the curious whiteness of its wings gathers to a ball in its beak, a quartzlike globe. An amethyst pupil completes the eye, which regards Williaus inquiringly but without much emotion. Then it begins to sing. (Williaus can tell it is the eye singing by the listening aspect of the bird.) It sings such lines as:

O Johnny O Johnny O

At the end of each song the noddy flies out of sight for a moment, bearing the eye, but soon comes back.

After a while Williaus asks if the eye could not sing an old song. The eye, with a look of surprise, consents to render *Come away, come sweet love.* But it insists on preceding each return to the old music with several popular songs.

By the end of the twenty-eighth day Williaus has given himself over to death. The lustrous voice fades. At a certain moment he becomes aware of a being close to him. He calls out, but hears only a rubbery clatter. Pulling the glove from his right hand, he stretches it towards the sound: a cold softness fills his palm. He leans farther: bones and silky whiskers, and a sweet whine. A new soft clatter, and the being's body moves against him. The seal puts his head on Williaus's lap who strokes it tenderly.

From time to time the seal moves away but usually Williaus can follow the flapping of its feet, or its short grunts. Once it goes far away but after a long hour returns. Williaus caresses it with happy relief. So doing he finds that the seal's smooth pelisse is rent with sores. His fingers explore the open wounds, the animal trembles at this touching. Williaus weeps, repeating Poor Roly, poor Roly, soothing its head. He weeps obliviously over the wet soft sores.

When the seal next starts to move away, Williaus pleads with it to stay. He cannot think how to keep it by him. Then remembering that music is attractive to seals, he begins to sing:

The first queen was a farmer's girl
With hair as yellow as hay,
She slept one night with the emperor
The emperor died next day

The third queen was a heathen
The fairest of all houris,
She danced for the devil's salva

vat

La lala

Williaus's body was carried by icedrift to the nearby edge of the polar pack, and thence, the ice breaking up, floated southward into the Atlantic on an iceberg. At summer's end it was observed by the passengers of Mr. Leigh Smith's yacht *Diana*. The body, recovered, was brought to Canada aboard that ship, and there Williaus's family took charge of it, returning with it to Los Angeles where the remains were burned.

GYPSIES

A soothing rush of waves had washed through the close of my recital. It was past midnight when the carriage stopped at the beach.

Someone outside opened the carriage-door and the beam of a flashlight entered. There was laughter from many men and women: I had been smoking a ninety-five-cent footlong cigar, and the light discovered me in a heap of smoke.

Such ash! said the man with the flashlight. My suit was thoroughly sprinkled with cigar droppings.

A sable silvered, I answered.

A silver Stewart?

Royally bearded! I said, feeling my stubbled chin.

Did you say: beheaded?

Purged by bitter hominy!

My questioner, helping me to the ground, laughed delightedly at my last answer. Taking my arm he led me towards the nearest of the campfires burning along the beach. We passed through a score of watching Gypsies.

When we had reached the fire my questioner shined his light on a trail of ashes pointing to my carriage. We were expecting you, he said, by this sign of the wind.

My polite smile revealed my skepticism. I have never seen such indignation. Protests from all sides persuaded me to submit to an experiment, although I feared that it would only bring new embarrassment.

From somewhere beyond the firelight a gypsy girl trundled a strange machine. It was made of two large flared cones of corrugated iron set one above the other. The lower one's base rested close to the ground on a ring of free wheels. The upper cone, joined to the lower by a tube in a way allowing each to revolve independently, was set at right angles to the first, its base, shut with a flat metal disc, facing outwards: it looked like the horn of some outsize Edison phonograph. The machine must have been seven feet high, and the diameter of the cones at their bases four feet; the short tube connecting them was only three inches thick at its narrowest point.

After unlocking three hooks on its surface, the girl swung out a large section of the lower cone together with the corresponding arc of the wheel-ring, and the machine was then pushed into position over the campfire, raked into a compact blazing pile of coals. During the moment the cone was open, I saw that its inner surface was covered with a spiral of close-set blackened vanes.

While the machine was being fetched, several Gypsy men had dug a shallow circular ditch around the fire, afterwards wetting it with buckets of seawater. The ring of wheels now rested in this trough of relatively firm sand.

All now drew back to a distance of ten yards from the fire, except for the girl who had fetched the machine. Turning the upper cone towards the sea, from which a steady wind blew, she removed the disc that sealed its base, and withdrew at once to the circle of watchers. The upper cone, which was evidently hollow, swung slightly to left and right before settling into place facing the wind. Slowly at first, the lower cone began to spin on its ring of wheels. A harsh whispering noise started, thickening and rising with the pace of the cone's gyration.

When the lower cone had reached a speed I would not have thought possible, so pronounced that its wheels had become a blur (it is true that the only light was that of the hidden fire), the machine's movements changed. The upper cone, previously immobile, started to revolve as the lower cone slowed. In a few seconds their roles had been reversed, the lower cone remaining still while the upper whirled violently. But I had barely accustomed myself to this transformation when with an ear-rending squeal all motion stopped, and the upper cone, which had come to its abrupt halt facing me, spouted a dazzling stream of coals. These when they fell rested for the merest instant in bright continuous lines: I read the word THESAURUS. At once the coals began to wink out, hissing damply. Five seconds after having seen the word I began doubting my eyes, confronted as I now was with only scattered embers, bearing as much resemblance to a word as a constellation to the legendary figure it portrays.

A shout from the Gypsies followed the word's appearance. I was ready enough to admit my error; but nobody was thinking any longer of that argument. Instead I was told that I must enter a contest with the leading men of the community. Since everyone was immediately busy preparing for this event, I was obliged to accept—especially as I had put myself so completely in the wrong.

I learned that the stake in the game was to be an extraordinary heirloom—in fact the treasure signified by "thesaurus"—but I was not yet told what it was. First of all I was to witness a special dance, a preliminary meant to emphasize the ritual character of the game.

We formed a new circle around the campfire. Music began. A crank victrola played the worn record of an old popular song. This music had a curious complement. Three women held strips of wetted white cloth and snapped them in turn, thus making a series of resounding retorts that possessed a certain rough element of pitch. The three strips were of unequal length: the middlesize one was only slightly longer than the shortest strip, while the longest was nearly its double. At long intervals that seemed to have no connection with the recorded music, the women would flick their cloths in rapid succession: first that of middle length, then the longest, finally the shortest.

Presently the dancers appeared—a handsome couple wearing only bathing suits, shaking with cold. The man crouched on the ground. The woman performed a solo during which she strewed over her partner bands of charred newspaper from a basket placed nearby. Once she had thoroughly covered the man and the ground around him, the woman withdrew. The man began to lift himself up. As he tried to shake off the papers, however, he became more and more entangled in them. I saw after a moment how the effect was achieved. A net had been laid on the spot where he had squatted, concealed by a light covering of sand, and he had picked it up when he rose. The strands of the net, furthermore, must have been dipped in strong glue, for the papers stuck to them firmly. After many elegant contortions, the dancer, wrapped from head to toe in a shroud of newsprint, fell onto the sand as if dead. The music's close marked the end of the dance.

It was then that my questioner with the flashlight—who turned out to be a chief—showed me the stake the Gypsies had put up for our game. It was nothing other than the "adze," as they called it—of course I pointed out that it wasn't an adze at all but a kind of short-handled halberd, or a large billhook. While they granted that it rather resembled such instruments, they insisted that it was an adze, and no ordinary one. The chief explained that the pictures engraved on its head portrayed the life of some ancient wonderqueen of theirs, from her birth to her burning. Then he and several other men discussed the last scene shown on it

—the one with moon, arrows, and fish—which they couldn't understand, still less agree on.

Next I was asked to put up *my* stake. I was at a loss. A hundred times the money I was carrying would not have bought the adze's gold, and then there was its symbolic value, which I gathered was the Gypsies' paramount reason for offering it up to chance. At last, reluctantly, I drew from my overcoat pocket my beloved dog Limnisse and announced my willingness to risk him. This extraordinary animal, bought three years previously at a secondhand dogstore on the Left Bank, was only four inches long and weighed only six ounces fed. But his brain, a marvel of nature, was equal to that of any Alsatian shepherd. When I bought him, a veteran circus roustabout had already trained him to perform such feats as measuring all distances from a foot to a mile with a margin of error of only one-sixteenth of an inch.

My hosts were delighted with Limnisse, and so the game finally started. It was played at another fire, over which a twenty-five gallon vat of water had been set to boil on a cast-iron tripod. The boiling water was funneled through a spigot into terracotta jars that, excepting a small hole left for this purpose, were entirely closed. The filled jars, borne on wooden trays by Gypsy girls, were passed in turn to the contestants who took them in their bare hands. Before setting his jar down, the contestant had to describe the scene molded on its top. If he dropped a jar, or put it on the ground without giving a fitting description, he was out of the game. When only two players remained, this procedure ended. Instead, the finalists joined in a kind of rhetorical contest, explaining the transcendent meaning of the scenes they had already described.

I was shown a sample jar top. Its picture was the same as the second one of the adze. The trick, the chief told me, is to use the fewest words possible, without sacrificing good usage or leaving out any part of the picture. In this case you might say, The lightningpucked thunder-hockeyists felled, our queen on cloud is admired.

I promised to do my best.

Looking back, I am sure that at least part of the game was prepared. Before I had five turns a dozen contestants—all but the chief and I—had managed either to drop their jars or to stutter unnaturally when their turn came. I can't remember half of what they did say, so I shall limit myself to us two finalists. I wasn't able, of course, to see the chief's jars: I can only report his words.

It was he who opened the game, saying of the first jar: A mast bears fruit for shipwrecked travelers.

I was nearly eliminated at my first turn. When I took the offered jar, in spite of all my inner preparations, its boiling heat blinded me. My vision fortunately cleared quickly enough to distinguish the crudely made image: a child was curled up, as if in the womb, within a circle on whose outer edge grew trees, shrubs and crops, all on fire. I said: The old world, burning, heralds the new one to be born.

The dialogue continued thus:

The chief: For gay gangs crossing, the sea's a velvet field.

Of a group of nine men on their knees, clubs laid aside, I said: Victorious Yankees pray for humility.

The chief: From the dead god's eye swarm fat swine.

My next scene showed two men, one of them looking in amazement at the other, who was chiseling at the bust of an old man set in the middle of a fence. I said of it: Confounding Brunelleschi, Donatello carves a venerable God from a fencepost.

The chief: Cool drink in hand, Somerset Maugham is gently toothdrilled. (I objected to "toothdrilled" but was overruled.)

Next I had to describe a picture in the upper half of which a pianist with fluttering hair regarded a cross, while below a plump bearded man engaged in tourney with an opponent in side-whiskers and velvet clothes. My description was: Brahms and Wagner joust for fame, but Liszt plays only for Jesus.

The chief: Joyous giants make, of bankcolumns, flutes.

And I, considering a prisoner who sang and played a mandolin while his guard stood by with ready whip, concluded: The punished liar sings a new song of truth.

The chief and I were now the only contestants, and we entered the final period of the game—the rhetorical summary of our descriptions. The chief spoke first.

The mast, and the flutes, the sea, the tooth, the eye, the eye, the tooth, the sea, the flutes, the mast: in in these there five all symbols it's we see have you a so glimpse meant into nicely the quite world here that but we Square all Washington yearn around for, of that anarchists paradise pleasant on the earth to of happens which as all literature prophets such from of Isaiah readers to to Vergil familiar to conception you a and bankcolumns me of have out sung—flutes that the world care in medical which painless pain and and comfortable fear as have well been as banished, luxurious where free plenty of is picture ensured touching and a when tooth we Maugham's will Mr. finally mention have to the forgot opportunity I to kaput promote world a old democratic the interest i.e. in god the dead fine the arts. Of is knowledge it is not that fitting eye that the this from new course age of should symbolically be proceeding first home heralded brought by easily the be miracle to that bacon saved the those by classic indicated victims as of notably pity, eat travelers to wrecked plenty on also a but barren all shore? To but available soon be plights advantages like negativistic theirs these will will have only been not forever foidermore banished—traverse the to sea desiring itself tread will baby lose merest its the periculousness, for being velvet transformed comfy to soft soft to comfy transformed velvet being for periculousness the its merest lose baby will tread itself desiring sea to the traverse. Banished foidermore forever—but enough! Glimpse so a you have see we it's symbols all five there, in the mast, the sea, the eye, the tooth, and the flutes!

There was considerable applause. In turn I rose to speak.

Eak! ay! irth! ine! ees! ost! er! ire! ird! ine! ew!

ladies gentlemen, tongue phrases. rhetoric day. man's glory earth, birth—birth goodness, light nature. men arms, knees strength humility's. sculptor glory god fencepost. tones flesh hands register. justice, liar (word) rack whip fire music bird. wonders seas swine, mercy wisdom flame—world.

is to wrap speak; say is to say keep; shown, tell—
began to shine; laid, fell, prayed, be; felt was made
spring; knew to stir confined; was (murdered) forced
to bear to sing; is bring to view; is;
weak another come stranger divine burning all brave
most mere weak upper merciful wretched twisted fair
true velvet milling blessed divine such new greater,
and and but when and, when and and or, or but
or but and,
in for on of, of to from with, to with with,
a the the, the the a th', the a the, the,
I me you, I you he, he he I,
plainly briefly there up down, but even not
like not,
my my, their their, their his, his his,
let, have been, shall, had, was,
what, what, who, that,
which?
—That I leave to you.

Cheers rose about the fire at my last words. There was no question as to who was winner, and the chief immediately congratulated me.

It is a new triumph, he said, of analytical poetry over descriptive prose. This reassured me—I was afraid my couplets might have passed unnoticed.

Dawn had begun to lighten the smoky beach when I started back to New York, with the awarded adze on my lap tied up in *Mirror* and string. Although I had won, it had been necessary for me to abandon my dog—evidently the stakes are exchanged in such cases, there being, according to those people, no such thing as a winner. So, giving him a last center slice of his favorite filet mignon, I said goodbye to Limnisse. It was the only bad moment of that diverting and exhausting night.

Several months later I sold the adze to Wayl, who had shown extraordinary interest in it, finally offering me more money than I could refuse.

Two o'clock in the morning had struck when the novelist finished his story. Tired, I suggested we meet another time to talk about the adze itself, and thanking him for his kindness, left.

MR. WAYL'S WILL

At six-thirty that morning a visitor woke me up: Beatrice Fod. Pale with fatigue, she nevertheless harangued me vigorously for several minutes. She wanted the adze, first claiming it as rightly hers and then, such arguments failing, offering me increasingly large amounts of money for it. Her final price was close to a million dollars—I have forgotten the exact sum because my mind at that time was aswim with sleep and surprise.

She was on her way out when another caller appeared, showing signs of the same tempestuous weariness: her brother Isidore.

Němgat jegů! he exclaimed.

Tsamp! she answered, shoving past him out the door. *Gego szegák egan egámpteggi egög segöl!*

Is Fod soon followed her, equally disappointed in his efforts to get the adze for himself.

In the afternoon papers I learned that Mr. Wayl had died the previous night. Soon afterwards I received a special delivery letter from Mr. Wayl's lawyers asking me to come to his house next morning to attend the reading of the dead man's will.

Although I had arrived before the appointed time, a remarkable number of people had already gathered in the familiar drawing-room, where the reading was to take place. Among them I recognized Mayor Groncz. He was, I later learned, the only person invited to the session outside the Fods, Miss Dryrein, and myself. I noticed many other distinguished figures: from medical circles, the surgeon Arbalast, who had once operated on Mr. Wayl's foot but was better known for his Harrow depth technique; the gynecologist White; Dr. Mallarmé, the woman who had revolutionized narcoanalysis with intravenous injections of "symbolic gin"; and Clematis, the "truth dentist"; two of Mr. Wayl's rare friends in the worlds of finance and business, Alexander Senfl of Medusa Natural Gas and Harvey Elliott of Milton Can, in earnest conversation with Jonathan Writch, the president of Blackwards, Reyrdin & Long; numerous leaders in the field of civic development—the chairman of the Parking Authority, the real estate king William Lemon, and the architect Miles Mazurovsky, among others; half-a-dozen aspiringly alert but unfamiliar lawyers under the wing of an anonymous redhaired dean; Philippa Stuart, elder of the Primal Rose Unitarians—the only religious figure of the gathering; among the military, Generals Peirce O'Toole, who had distinguished himself during the last war in reducing the "pocket bulge," and Quogue, the "Bremen Monster"; Admiral "Rock" Hatter, and Captain Hershey, who had never become admiral (despite a brilliant record) because of his lifelong skepticism towards the torpedo; several politicians besides Mayor Groncz—Governor Gold of Delaware, author of a book (*Mass or Mess?*) that had angered many Catholics, Senator Cousins, whose promising legal career was ending in political mediocrity, and Senator Autobustard, the royalist; many writers and journalists, including the poet Felix Hughes (*The Artifice of Order*), "Sylvester" of *Field & Stream*, and the cartoonist Flamingo Stahl, for whom the epithet "vitriolic" had been worn to new thinness; from the theatrical world, Laetitius Scott, the backer of *Invitation to a Sabbath*, an avant-garde sleeper that had recently opened on Fire Island; Violet Colt, directress of the China Co.'s film subsidiaries, whose stinginess was legendary; Archibald Moon, then at the height of his powers as Judas in *The White Net;* and his wife Anna Joyce who had distinguished herself in a role of "trying piety" playing opposite him; the art dealer Seaward Blackmaster and his principal client, Edward Emord, both probably hoping to learn how Mr. Wayl had disposed of Watteau's *Blue Friend;* Duane Greene; the museum director Rudolph Sweenson Barjohn; such members of the musical world as Demuro Bangcraft and Reobard Mitrostone; and a few of the many painters once patronized by Mr. Wayl—de Crook (who had painted his "purple portrait"), Huffing (the exponent of *arte brutta*), Rauschwald and Litotes.

The consensus of this assembly was that Mr. Wayl's fortune exceeded three billion dollars.

The Fods, accompanied by Miss Dryrein, at last took their seats (Beatrice shouting Vampires! Vampires! as she crossed the room.) A pale attorney, flanked by bespectacled aides, read the will behind a massive table placed in front of the high windows that looked on the conservatory.

> I, GRENT OUDE WAYL, of the City, County, and State of New York, do make, publish, and declare this to be my Last Will and Testament, hereby revoking any and all Wills and Codicils heretofore made by me.
>
> FIRST: I direct that all my just debts and funeral expenses be paid by my executrix as soon as possible after my decease, provided that the following procedure be adhered to:
>
> (1) That the organist of St. James's Church, Madison Avenue and 71st Street, Manhattan, choose a suitable musical composition to accompany the departure of my remains to their place of burial; that the score of this composition (notes, rests, clefs, key and time signatures, and all indications of speed, phrasing and dynamics) be reproduced at fifteen times its printed size in the form of pancakes; and that these cakes be obligatorily eaten by any and all such persons who attend the reading of this my Last Will and

Testament, excepting those specifically invited thereto. (In the event of non-compliance with this provision, I have instructed my faithful servant Miss Gabrielle Dryrein, of 2980 Valentine Avenue, The Bronx, to give to the press all information kept in my private files concerning liable parties.)

(2) That I be buried with my ninety-nine-year custombuilt Fil Pathétique fob watch, this watch to be set at Greenwich time and placed in my left waistcoat pocket immediately prior to the funeral service.

(3) That my coffin be taken from St. James's Church at eleven o'clock of the Monday morning following my death, on an open cart drawn by two gray donkeys, and that the itinerary of the procession be as follows: Madison Avenue from 71st until 59th Street; Fifth Avenue from 59th until 50th Street; Park Avenue from 50th until 34th Street; and thence to my residence where my remains are to be buried. (In the event of non-compliance with this provision, the following article of this Will is automatically annulled.)

SECOND: I give and bequeath to Mr. Lambeth Groncz, of Gracie House, Gracie Square, Manhattan, such land as I possess in the City of New York, notably a park of three acres adjoining my present residence, 475 East 34th Street, Manhattan.

THIRD: I give and bequeath to my faithful servant Miss Gabrielle Dryrein, of 2980 Valentine Avenue, The Bronx:

(1) The sum of Two Hundred and Fifty Thousand Dollars ($250,000.);

(2) The sum of One Hundred Thousand Dollars ($100,000.) to be distributed at her discretion

among those who are, or who have been, in her service;

(3) All of my personal effects, including clothing, jewelry, silver, furniture, furnishings, books, pictures and ornaments.

FOURTH: All the rest, residue and remainder of my property, real, personal and mixed, wheresoever situate, including property of any description of which I may die seized or possessed, of which I may have power to dispose, over which I may have power of appointment, and in and to which I may be in any manner interested or entitled, I give, devise and bequeath to such person as has in his possession a golden adze hereunder described and who is able to provide a satisfactory explanation of its meaning, purport, uses and significance, now and at all times, the said explanation to be verified by my executrix or by such executors as she may appoint according to the answers given by any qualifying person to the following three questions:

1) When was a stone not a king?
2) What was *La Messe de Sire Fadevant?*
3) Who shaved the Old Man's Beard?

The description of the adze followed. Read with rising voice by the shamefaced lawyer, it was quickly drowned in a clamor of shock and disappointment.

Mr. Wayl was never buried at all. His instructions were faithfully carried out, even to the eating of the transcribed music. The organist at St. James's, who had planned a twenty-nine minute *Tragic Rhapsody* of Widor, was warned of the consequences and changed to a unison version of *O God Our Help in Ages Past;* so that the forced feeders had only twenty-eight notes to swallow between them, and—the hymn being all in wholenotes and halfnotes—hollow ones at that.

The procession following the funeral service caused the worst traffic jam in New York's history, and Mayor Groncz might have been impeached for having allowed such a situation to arise, if he had not announced his intention of giving the land he had inherited to the city. The drawn cart had completed about three quarters of the itinerary when, at the corner of Park Avenue and Forty-ninth Street, in the midst of a throng of the idle, the curious and the infuriated, the coffin exploded. Little harm was done to bystanders by the explosion itself, since the coffin was made of welded steel; but the panic resulting from the noise and the strange rain of white petals that fell across the crowded intersection led to one death and many injuries. Investigators concluded, after considering the powdery contents of the coffin, that Mr. Wayl's watch had triggered the tragic detonation.

A VISIT TO THE FODS

When was a stone not a king? What was *La Messe de Sire Fadevant?* Who shaved the Old Man's Beard? When was a stone ever a king? Who was Sire Fadevant? What old man? To approach the questions on which my inheritance depended, others had to be answered first. I tackled the problem at once.

Besides study and research at official sources for information about the so-called adze, I thought it well to visit all of Mr. Wayl's surviving relatives. Even if they refused to cooperate with me, I might indirectly glean clues for my search.

These relatives were, besides the Fods: Allen Cavallo in New York; Xavier Purkinje in Paris; and the Voe-Doge brothers, Gore and Eftas, in London.

I first went to the Fods. Each received me with surprising friendliness. My impression was that after a short spell of appetency they had lapsed into wearied resignation.

Beatrice's and Isidore's histories were curious. Both had been involved in notorious medical scandals, following which Mr. Wayl had taken them under his protection. They lived in one of his properties, a thin four-storey house on West Fifty-fifth Street that had been divided into two apartments.

At the age of thirty Beatrice, a budding professor of gynecology at Johns Hopkins, had hit on an unprecedented solution to the problem of birth control. She had discovered (and, with the help of four thousand volunteer college and high school students of every class, race and region in the country, tested) a position for sexual intercourse in which conception was impossible. Her position, furthermore, provided maximum satisfaction for both partners in the sexual act, incidentally lowering the average age at which vaginal orgasm was first experienced from twenty-two to sixteen and a half years.

The consequences of Beatrice's discovery seemed potentially historic; but no sooner had she published the first results of her long labor than she was attacked on several sides by forces too strong for her to meet. Several drug firms had at that time invested seven-figure sums in developing an oral contraceptive. Seconded by the Federal Government, which planned to use the monopoly of the new chemical as a diplomatic weapon (with the Catholic powers of Europe as well as the populous Afro-Asian states), these firms undertook to stifle Beatrice's good work. They contributed vast amounts of money to every conceivable religious denomination, abroad as well as at home, thereby achieving an intersectarian harmony unique in history. The propaganda was so clamorous that the few organizations favoring Beatrice's cause were obliged to abandon her to save themselves.

Meanwhile the government managed to have a law enacted making punishable by life imprisonment at hard labor anyone who published a book or pamphlet without depositing at the Library of Congress the three copies necessary to obtain copyright. Beatrice had neglected to do this. She had published her findings privately and inconspicuously, in the hope that by so acting (and also by omitting a description of the coital position she had invented) her discovery would gain an easier entrance into the realm of public information; for she had foreseen an adverse reaction. Instead, all copies of her pamphlet save the first few she had sent out were confiscated by the police, while she herself became guilty of a severely punishable crime. A bargain had been proposed to her: if she kept silence in the future, she would not be prosecuted. Exhausted and frightened, she accepted, and now lived under the eyes of federal agents who investigated her most trivial relations. For a while she had hoped that the students who had tested her theory would give it to the world, and indeed some of them tried. (A debased version of her discovery—the so-called Lombard Rhythm—had a certain brief success.) But so many positions had been used to make the experiment statistically exact that nobody was sure which was the true one, and a great confusion resulted, bringing much disappointment and, finally, the loss of her secret.

Isidore Fod's misfortune had come about at much the same time as his sister's, but in a way quite different. He had been working for the Bengali government on a sanitation project when an epidemic of tracheitic plague broke out in a remote mountain plateau of the province. Neither remedy nor vaccine for this disease existed; and even if they had, the difficulty of delivering them rapidly to the infested region seemed insuperable—besides its remoteness, its topography rendered it inaccessible to truck or plane.

Isidore Fod solved the double problem with an ingenuity that approached genius. After growing a culture of the plague bacteria, he discovered an effective although partial antidote to their virulence in the venom of the local *ischnogaster* wasp: the wasp-poison scotched the bacteria without completely killing them. In a few days Isidore performed a rapid series of tests that showed that a person injected with a mixture of germ culture and wasp poison became, at least temporarily, immune to the plague without suffering any ill effects. Because of the emergency, the state government immediately authorized Isidore to proceed, without further testing, in making vaccinations with his new serum.

To lessen the difficulty of delivering the vaccine, Isidore set up his medical station at English Bazar, the city nearest the stricken area. There he had a six-foot-square shallow cement pool made, and planted it with five thousand golf-tees obtained from the city golf club (a fortunate survivor of India's independence). The tees were fixed so that their cups were at a uniform height of five-eighths of an inch from the bottom of the pool. The tee cups were then filled with a thick solution of sugar, the pool with a half-inch of bacteria culture, and the whole was enclosed with screens provided with two opposing apertures. Every available truck and car had meanwhile been commandeered to scour the countryside for *ischnogaster* nests (gargoyle-like masses familiar to any traveler who has crossed the Bengal plains). Tens of thousands were brought to Isidore's station, where their occupants were dropped in batches onto the prepared enclosed pool. The great majority of wasps at once descended to the sweet-baited golf-tees. As each one sucked up his portion of syrup, the stinging tip of his curved tail dipped into the bacteria culture that mounted almost to the edge of the golf-tee top. When sated, the wasp would soon proceed through the prepared exit into a portable screen cage, whither the swarming sound of his trapped fellows drew him. The pool was periodically emptied and the supplies of sugarwater and culture replenished, while the cages of vaccine-bearing wasps were taken to the airport to be loaded on ready planes. As soon as each plane had its consignment, it took off for the plague area where, flying low over the inhabited points, it freed its enraged cargo. The effect of this operation was later described in a tribute that the poet Hānsām Dās wrote for Isidore Fod:

The jackal cries, the *kokil* sings in leafy wonder
And behind the wattles babes peer at the sky.

Ah, swarm of gold, searing pain,
Blessing of the worn-out year!
Come, I am but a *champa* flower that longs for
the hornet's kiss.

An estimated two million wasps were loosed on an area of four hundred and fifty square miles inhabited by eighty thousand people. Some sixty thousand were stung, and of these only thirty-five died of the plague. Over two thousand had died prior to the period of vaccination, while several hundred of those not stung subsequently perished of the disease, which was several weeks waning. Isidore's assumption that the wasps' stings would effect a safe but potent mixture of culture and poison at the moment they pierced the skin turned out to be right, as had all his other guesses.

For the next eight months Isidore was a worldwide hero. He chose, modestly, to stay in Bengal until the work for which he had been originally hired was completed. This decision nearly cost him his life. The next summer the plague returned to the same mountain region with new fury, and this time Isidore's airlift was of no use. Setting out with his assistants to investigate the plague area, he reached it after a fortnight's travel by mule. He soon made two significant discoveries: one, that his vaccine had only a short-lived effectiveness; the other, that the wasps he had dropped the year before had become breeders of the plague. A mutation in the bacteria had produced a strain that not only remained unaffected by wasp poison but flourished in the bodies of the wasps. Left behind wherever the wasps fed, these bacteria now had every local insect for a carrier. The recrudescence of the plague spared hardly a household in all the region.

Before the cold weather finally ended the epidemic, it had killed thirty thousand. With admirable honesty Isidore informed the Bengali government and the press of his findings, and thus fell overnight into such local and international disgrace that he gave up his professional work altogether, finally coming to New York to live on Mr. Wayl's bounty and his own regrets.

Questioned, Beatrice Fod appeared even more ignorant concerning the adze than I. There was evidently little chance that either she or her brother would ever have the time to learn any more about it, in case they decided to go after the enigmatic inheritance themselves. In return for supporting them, Mr. Wayl had made them each accept a trying obligation, that of observing and noting everything that the other did. The ordeals they had passed through had left them, understandably, more than a little suspicious, and their suspiciousness had only grown with exercise, so that now —despite Mr. Wayl's death—their mutual spying was a terrific obsession.

Thus Beatrice Fod, while answering me with brief courtesies, refused to discuss anything at length but a mysterious flatiron that Isidore kept on his mantelpiece. Why did he have it? Did he ever use it? If he did use it, what did he use it for? Possible answers to these ridiculous questions filled my ears for over an hour, while I gazed stupidly about the living-room, studded—like the entire apartment—with grotesque pointed furniture. (Not a chair, shelf or sofa whose corners did not extrude in exaggerated tapering acuteness, causing in the beholder an irremediable awareness of impending pain. Beatrice did explain that she had taking up singing as a recent hobby and that such furnishings set off her voice better than any other.)

I had even less success with Isidore, for he refused to speak at all and sat with his forefinger at his lips in a listening posture, as if waiting for revelatory noises from his sister's apartment. I saw the flatiron on his mantelpiece but never learned its significance, or even if it had any.

•

OTHER PRISONERS

Allen Cavallo, whom I visited next, was the grandson of Mr. Wayl's second stepfather, not a blood relation; he was therefore without expectations as to the inheritance and I had little hope that he would give me any useful information, since Mr. Wayl had hardly known him. My hopes were further limited by knowing that "Al" Cavallo was a notorious gang boss. Only Mayor Groncz's intervention enabled me to visit him in the Astoria Agrarians' Hospital, where he was kept in a private and indeed secret room of the psychiatric department.

Shortly before, Cavallo had disappeared mysteriously from public view—all that one knew was that he was under arrest. At the hospital I found out what had happened.

The gangster had learned the previous year of a newly discovered cactus that grew in the foothills of the Hoggar. Its spines were powerfully narcotic, discouraging the animals of that desolate land from eating the juicy flesh of the plant. As the toxic properties of these spines made them similar in their effect to morphine, it was at first hoped that they could be used medically; but the difficulties of extracting the active chemical proved excessive. Cavallo had a sample of the plant sent to him; and testing the spines on a number of his morphine customers, he had found that they satisfied the cravings of the most addicted. He had also discovered an unguessed advantage to the spines: carried as toothpicks, they freed their possessor from the risk of arrest and the need of concealment. An addict wanting his stuff could publicly clean his teeth with a spine, unobtrusively pricking his gums until happy. The spines soon gained the nickname of "Hoggar-mothers."

Cavallo ordered a large quantity of the cactus and set up a plant import business as a front. The first shipment was unloaded one summer night at a Brooklyn wharf under Cavallo's personal supervision. Checking a loaded truck before it drove off, he had the tragic misfortune to fall—or, some say, be pushed—among the four-foot-deep green bulbs. Lightly covered in that season, every part of his body was pierced by the drug-laden thorns. Before he could be retrieved, he had been hopelessly stricken by a massive injection of narcotic sap.

Under constant medical care since that night, at first among his colleagues, later, arrested, at the hospital where I saw him, Cavallo was an inhuman and pitiful sight. He was insane, and in unremitting pain as well. The narcotic, absorbed in a quantity that could never be eliminated, caused his skin to shrink perpetually. Hardly a day passed without an incision being needed in some part of his body to keep it from being squeezed dry by this terrible pressure. The incisions left him covered with long halfhealed wounds inadequately fitted with grafts from volunteers or with plastic skin. Between his shrieks and raving laughs he sometimes used to cry out, By these stripes we are healed! These were the only words he spoke. He died a few weeks after my visit to him.

About this time the efforts I had made to find information concerning the adze yielded their first result. A letter from the Customs Bureau informed me that they had located the records of its arrival in America. The shipment had been made from Alloa, in Scotland, by a New York export-import company that had long been out of business, so that it would be impossible to find out the actual persons who had sent and received it.

But even this meager information seemed a windfall to me, and I decided to go to Scotland and see if there I could not trace the adze back to its origins. At the same time the trip would give me a chance to visit Mr. Wayl's remaining relatives.

In Paris a few weeks later, I made arrangements to

call on M. Purkinje, a distant cousin of Mr. Wayl's on his mother's side. He, too, was in the hands of the police, as he had been ever since the failure of the Panarchist Uprising of 1911. Together with his fellow agitators, Martinotti and Rackham the Red, he had passed most of his life in the political wing of Les Innocents, France's largest prison. Its director, M. Molini-Stucky, who had promptly granted my request for a visit, related while leading me to the prisoner's quarters the events that had brought Purkinje there.

The Panarchist revolt, he began, was one of the cleverest attempts at generalized subversion that our country (rich in similar exploits) has ever known. Imagination and efficacy characterized its choice of political doctrine, while its technique of psychological preparation and its tactics for making the uprising a success were no less ingenious.

The Panarchist doctrine was known as *éclairagisme*. Designed to appeal to the universal predilection for oversimplified and seemingly practical ideas, it reduced all social ills to one—darkness—, and it advocated one cure, summed up in the slogan *Tout l'Espace Éclairé!* According to this theory the amount of light available to a person in all the phases of his daily life determined his moral, psychic and intellectual wellbeing. It was accordingly the obligation of the state to ensure first of all that each individual have the same amount of light as every other, and secondly that this amount be as great as possible. The Panarchists claimed that the discovery of electric light—which you should remember was fairly recent and so made the theory especially attractive—permitted both these obligations to be easily realized. They consequently advocated that a light quota be established on a space-person basis; that all those persons required to live or work in an insufficiently lighted space be given larger windows and increased electric lighting; and that those persons whose illumination exceeded the quota have their window surface reduced and their lighting fixtures confiscated correspondingly.

But the Panarchists' program, reiterated in their daily paper *Le Soleil de Paris*, soon left theoretical *éclairagisme* to the debates of pundits and focused on livelier issues such as the abolition of the *minuterie* or the construction of giant mirrors to introduce sunlight and moonlight to the narrower streets. And in a few years, by dint of exploiting this rudimentary idea, the Panarchist Party (PP) gained a respectable following.

The party's aim had been revolutionary from the start, although this was not openly acknowledged until the inability of successive governments to provide the lighting reforms demanded had been demonstrated to the masses. When they felt that a fit moment for action had come, the Panarchist leaders began their scheduled "psychological preparatory movement," based on the principle of *psychomimie*. Their idea was to accustom the populace to revolutionary gestures so that it would be conditioned to perform, or at least tolerate, such gestures when the crisis occurred. For this reason, during the month preceding the date chosen for the revolution, Parisians were offered a number of unusual spectacles. Buildings made of paper were set up on sidewalks and ignited by men whose smiles were a plea for the joys of arson. Other men and women, wearing like smiles, made piles of bricks and stones resembling little barricades. Fairstands were opened in all the working quarters of the city where one could, free of charge, shoot or throw hard balls at dummies of policemen and soldiers. These efforts at persuasion were naturally kept within careful bounds, to avoid official sanction; they were nonetheless everywhere to be seen.

It is hard to say how effective *psychomimie* was in its application, for the Panarchist leaders were all under arrest before they had time to exploit its effect. But that effect, if we are to judge by the climax of the campaign, was probably all they hoped for.

It so happened that the national hockey championships were to be played in Paris on the evening picked for the Panarchist outbreak. A huge crowd was to attend the game; so were several notables, among them the ministers of culture and of agriculture. The Panarchists, finding they could enlist both teams for their plan, decided to make the *Palais Esquimau* the starting-point of the mass rioting on which they counted. When the second period of the game began, revolutionaries replaced the official referees and, after haranguing the startled but far from hostile crowd, ordered the players to proceed as planned. The two government ministers, who had been prevented from leaving, were brought onto the ice and trussed up, their knees against their chests, their feet against their buttocks. The hockey players thereupon began a mock game with these human bundles as pucks; they pushed and passed them around the rink with the large scrapers used to clear off the ice. After their miserable excellencies had been with much jocularity scuttled into the goalnets, Martinotti, the Panarchist in charge, made a rousing speech to the spectators, pouring contempt on the government whose representatives had been so thoroughly humiliated. The crowd, responding enthusiastically, swarmed out of doors intending to do all the mischief it could; but the police (who by now were on the offensive) were waiting for it, and it was quickly dispersed.

The failure of the revolution was really a matter of luck. The main objective of the plotters was a series of "temporary assassinations" that were to destroy the leadership of the police and of the army divisions stationed in or near the capital. Here again the Panarchists showed singular flair. As you may know, Paris then had two telephone systems, one that of a private company, the other that of the Postal Service. The latter was gradually replacing the former; but at that particular time the transition was not completed and both systems existed side by side. The revolutionaries' plan, carried out successfully in the majority of cases, was to call their victims on both phones simultaneously—I should perhaps mention that the phones were invariably next to one another, since the Postal Service had taken advantage of the private company's wiring scheme to install its own. Then, through a clever use of conversation—worked out experimentally with great thoroughness prior to use—the person answering was induced to hold both phones to his ears at the same time. At this foreseen moment, explosive noises of nearly a hundred decibels were sent over the two wires to produce in the unsuspecting hearer a striking manifestation of the Allanic-Culajod Effect. This left him senseless for a few hours.

As I've already said, this clever procedure succeeded

in most cases. But, unfortunately for the Panarchists, the prefect of police, their main target, was completely missed. He had planned to spend the evening of the would-be coup doing research on Louise Labé, on whom he was an authority; and he ignored his butler's announcement that he was demanded urgently on both phones. Shortly afterwards an alert aide informed him in person of the Panarchists' doings, and the prefect was then able, despite the decimation of the upper ranks of the police, to create a provisional hierarchy that soon had its forces mobilized. Before the night was over it was the Panarchist leadership that was inoperative, with two hundred of its members in jail. As you know, some of them aren't out yet. You will now see what they have become, these men who were, you must agree, exemplars of shrewdness and daring.

We had stopped in front of a door whose metal weight did not prevent our hearing, from its far side, a noise like the sighing of profound flutes. A guard unlocked the door, and we passed through. We entered a pleasant suite of cells, whose windows held, instead of bars, boxes of geraniums that sparkled in the morning sun; whose floors were thickly rugged; and whose *art nouveau* furnishings were elegant and luxurious. Three men reclined in capacious armchairs around a pale table on which had been set three glasses and a bottle of plain red wine. The men sat motionless, only sipping their wine from time to time. They uttered perpetual dovelike sounds. I recognized Purkinje, whose high cheekbones still retained a certain nobility in his face's damp fleshiness.

M. Molini-Stucky addressed Purkinje, shaking him by the shoulders. He succeeded in making him look once at me; but not for a moment did his sighing falter, and the revolutionary's eyes soon wandered to the sunlight that was filling the street below. Spreading his arms in hopelessness, the director led the way out; and I was obliged, empty-handed again, to leave Mr. Wayl's cousin and his comrades droning to themselves at their cheerful window that overlooked the Rue Affres de Guillaume.

I left for England next morning and a few days later payed a visit to the Voe-Doge brothers at their apartment in Chelsea. Shown into their drawing-room at the fixed hour, I found them engaged in furious argument.

Lop oh oh kop, Eftas was saying, yoppo you boploppo oh dopyop foppo ohlop, ee voppeenop top hoppo you gop hop mopyop boppeye roptop hop moppay yop hoppay voppee poproppee coppee doppeedop yoppo you ropsop bopyop oh noplopyop foppo roptop yoppo noppee soppee coppo nopdop sop, top hoppay top eyesop sopyou fopfop eye coppeye eenoptop toppo Aesop top aybop loppeye sop hop moppee aysop ee lopdoppee rop boproppo top hoppeerop, aynopdop roppeye gop hoptop fopyou loppy ay rop lop.

Naraguts tarago yaragou, baragag-haraguead, answered Gore: twaraguins aragare twaraguins aragand naragueitharaguer haragas praraguiaragoraraguitaraguy. Faragurtharaguermaragore araguit's caragommaragon knaragowlaraguedge tharagat yaragou paragayed Faragatharaguer Daraguldaragoon, wharago daraguelaraguivaraguered paragoor Maragummy, tharaguë praraguice aragof faraguive haragundraraguëd plaraguenaragararaguy araguindaragulgearaguenceafunction araguës tarago saragupparagort yaragour claragaim aragof baraguëaraguing faraguirstbaragorn.—Crapper, a glass of port for our guest.

Roppo toptop eenop coproppay popyoulop oh you sop you nopbop roppo top hoppee roplopyop loppeye Aesop!

Narago! aragand wharagat's maragore, Gore added, aragaccaragordaraguing tarago yaragou-knaragow-wharago tharaguere araguis narago daragoubt tharagat Aragui sharagould haragave baragueen maragade Araguearl aragof Maragar, aragand tharagat araguin faragact Aragui *aragam* tharaguë Aragearl.

Eyemop top hoppee Araguearl aragof Maragar!

Araguï'm tharaguë E ayroplop oh fop Moppayrop!

After three glasses of this jargon I took my leave. I did so with singular regret. A painting, signed only with the initials F. N., hung over the drawing-room fireplace; its composition was identical with the third scene of the adze—the supposed sanctification of the saint by Jesus. To my surprise, the brass plate on the bottom of its frame read: *The Crowning of the King*. The maid who accompanied me to the door assured me that no matter how long I might wait, the brothers would never condescend to speak of the picture—the only subject they ever discussed was that of their present argument.

I learned some time later that Gore was the celebrated "Tock" Voe-Doge, who used to fly his Spitfire during the Battle of Britain wearing the clothes he thought proper for the time of day. He once destroyed six German planes between ten and eleven in the morning dressed in scarlet shantung pajamas, sealskin slippers, and a skyblue cashmere dressing-gown with silver piping.

THE CUSTOMS HOUSE (I)

That very night I took the train for Edinburgh, going on the following morning to Alloa. There I went straight to the customs office. My inquiries regarding the adze led me through many bureaux; and it was not until late afternoon that the relevant papers were found. I was then informed that the adze had been registered for export not at Alloa itself, but at a special customs house near Alva, a small town three miles to the north.

Early the following morning I therefore set out anew. Reaching Alva by bus, I walked the last mile to the customs house through wet fields. After about a quarter of an hour I heard a sound of voices singing, and they grew louder as I followed my path. To my surprise the music was a partsong written in antique counterpoint, poignant and smooth. The moving voices hid the text, and it was only at the end of the verses that I caught the words of a chordal refrain:

White silver, blue,
Sweet silver, silver sweet!

The autumn mist kept me from seeing whence this music came, until I found myself a few yards from a building above whose door hung a worn sign, *The Customs House of Alva.* Fixed above this was a sixteen-inch loudspeaker pouring forth, with uncanny realism, the madrigal I had been listening to.

The door had neither bell nor knocker, only a risp, and this stuck. My efforts to work it, however, showed the door to be unlatched and I passed through it into a sad small entrance of drab wood, containing only a table with dried-out inkwells and an empty chair. Certain slight sounds from an adjacent room came through a frail door directly beyond the table. I knocked, had no answer, tried the knob, opened the door and entered a larger room. At first I could not see how large, for the air was suffused with plumes and tiers of smoke bluetinged with the illumination of a sizable skylight; but once my eyes had grown used to the foggy atmosphere I discovered a kind of gallery in front of me, ten yards wide and forty deep, its windowless walls lined with shelves, and its floor piled with cases and boxes. In a far corner a small area had been partitioned off, and a bright electric glow came through its open door.

Several weaker, unshaded lamps stood in the center of the room, and by their light a dozen officials were reading. They wore purplish military uniforms with visored caps and riding boots, but their bearing was unsuited to their dress. On a ring of overstuffed sofas they slackly sprawled, each smoking a long fair *regalia* which when sufficiently reduced was replaced from a litter of open cigarboxes that lay among them on the floor—no doubt seized contraband. In the same fashion each official exchanged from time to time the book he read for one chosen from a jumbled crateful at his feet. A side of the bookcrate had the word *Confiscated* stenciled on it.

None of the customs officials took any notice of me when I came in, and when I asked for their attention they did not even look up. Occasionally they spoke a word or two to each other in the soft speech of the country. After I had watched them restlessly for ten minutes, one finally raised himself languorously from his comfort (scratching his jowls with a piercing sound of grated fat and bristle), and approached me. He asked me my business in a brutal but imperfect German accent put on for the occasion. I presented an explanatory note from the Alloa customs office. He pointed to an empty place on one of the sofas and motioned to me to sit there, then disappeared with my letter into the partitioned corner at the end of the room.

I followed his order. Despite the cigarsmoke, richer than ever, I now saw that the customs officials were all reading imperial quarto books, whose covers, entirely taken up with photographs, had no title. A sample from the crate on the floor revealed this title-page: The Complete Erotic Poetry/of/Asafu Zir-jamah/ Translated into English Verse/by/Julia Tilt/volume LXXVIII/Printed for the Translatrix/by/The Felicitas Press/Schruns. Leafing through I observed that the poems' line endings proceeded in alphabetical order from one work to the next, from the opening limerick (with the rhymes *mamma*, *pyjama*, *diva*, *Godiva*, *Dalai Lama*) to the closing sestina (*Liz*, *fuzz*, *buzzbuzz*, *Oz*, *jazz*, *Alcatraz*).

The photographs adorning the covers—one on the front, one on the back—were peculiar to each volume. The sample I examined indicated no clear relation between picture and text. On one of its sides, a tall bottle labeled *Bols* stood on a table near an ivory mallet. A slight protuberance appeared in the smooth glass about halfway up one side of the bottle, and here the liquid within, otherwise clear, had a certain opaqueness. The other cover showed a multilevel safe, whose drawers, fitted with combination locks, bore such labels as: Lust, Hunger, Alcoholism, Filial Love.

The book read by the official who sat beside me was illustrated with similarly insignificant photographs.

I could see, on the front cover to my right, a room whose diplomaed walls suggested a doctor's office. It was empty except for an armchair made out of wax; this chair was indented in every part by the marks of human teeth that had bitten hard into its substance. The back of the same volume portrayed another room, furnished as a salon. I cannot be sure of my interpretation, but it seemed that an abstract mosaic embedded in one of the walls had begun to proliferate—the other walls, part of the floor, and even much of the furniture were covered with a layer of tesserae that appeared to be spreading over them like ambitious grass.

Many minutes passed with no sign of the official who had borne off my letter. My gaze, straying across the shelves of books that stretched the length of one wall, stopped at a sign reading: *Seized at the request of the Earl of Mar.* I wondered how any private person, even noble, could exercise such a power. I asked my neighbor, who had an odd B-shaped mole on his cheek, if he would satisfy my curiosity on this point—and to my surprise he assented. More, my question roused several other lazing officials.

Nine of them gathered round me. Under their glittering visors their faces looked soft and old and filled with the resignation of old barflies.

This custms hous (one said) was bult in the sixtenth centry to tax the metl producd by the Silvr Glen of Alva, whch blonged then, as now, to the Erls of Mar.

The Arls (the second haltingly took up) in llowing his ax to be mposed on the roduce of heir orkings, tipulated hat in eturn hey be iven ertain rivileges.

The' wer firs of al (the third whisperingly intervened) themselve to exercis thei contro on al o th good comin into thi regio of Scotlan, fixin and levyin tariff as the' chos.

Furthermo (the fourth scratching his pate added) they were allow to appoi the officia, with the ki's conse, who were to administ the roy levi at the sa ti as their o.

Nw by and by (the fifth gently crowed) thes appointmnts acquird a certan importanc, and som of thm wer bestowd to rewrd exceptionl servics as hereditar offics.

Whn (the sixth darkly confided) the mnes of the Slver Gln wre bandoned, the ffices cntinued, nd hve dne so dwn to the prsent—all of us are in trth dscendants of thse nble srvants whm the Arls of Mr nce hnored wth the pst of cstms fficial.

O coure (the seventh screechily exclaimed) ou dutie hae no the importane the' ha i the ol day!

By the ay (the eighth characteristically asked) id ou ear the usic his orning? Hat is an od ustom, ideed an obligation, iposed on us oficers—we are upposed eery orning, on oening the ustoms-ouse, to ing the *Ymn to Ilver* omissioned from ome aonymous Elizabethan omposer to elebrate the ine.

Fr sm tm nw (the ninth mutteringly concluded) wv fnd it bttr—mr btfl as wll as plsntr fr us—to tk dvntg of the ltst tchnlgcl prgrss in prfrmng ths tsk.

Thanking all the officials for their helpfulness, I crossed the room to look over the books the Earls of Mar had thought necessary to suppress.

Among them were such varied titles as:

Samuel Pegge, the younger, *Curialia miscellanea; anecdotes of old times*
Leonard Wright, *The hunting of Antichrist*
Wright's chaste wife, The
Daniel Featley, *The fisher catcht in his own net*
Edward Blount, *The hospital of incurable fools*
Thomas Pearson, *Infidelity; its aspects, causes, and agencies*
Thomas Campbell, *Gertrude of Wyoming*
Mary E. Braddon, *Only a clod*

Robert Baron, *The Cyprian academie*
Sir James M. Barrie, *When a man's single*
William Gouge, *The dignitie of chivalrie*
George Peele, *The honor of the garter*
Susanna Centlivre, *A bold stroke for a wife*
Frank Barrett, *The sin of Olga Zassoulitch*
Richard Kearton, *Wild life at home*
John Stuart Blackie, *Lays of the highlands*
Henry Rowlands, *Mona Antiqua restaurata*
Nicholas Rowe, *The biter, a comedy*
John Hunter, *The natural history of the human teeth*
Thomas Hall, *Funebria florae; the downfall of May-games*
Nathaniel Hawthorne, *The scarlet letter*
Robert Greene, *The historie of Orlando furioso*
Robert Records, *The urinal of physick*
Bert Morton, *The poet's office*
Mrs James W. Loudon, *Botany for ladies*
Thomas Bayly, *Herba parietis, or the wall-flower*
Henry Peacham, the younger, *Minerva Britanna, or a garden of heroical devises*
Henry Stubbe, *Rosemary and Bayes: or, animadversions upon a treatise called The rehearsall trans-prosed*
John Florio, *Queen Anna's new world of words*
Ralph D. Wornum, *Analysis of ornament*
Hesba Stretton, *Through a needle's eye*
Bp Edward Reynolds, *The rich man's charge*
Jonathan Slick, *High life in New York*
Hamon L'Estrange, *Americans no Jewes*
Hamon L'Estrange, *The alliance of divine offices*
Richard B. Kimball, *Undercurrents of Wall Street*
Samuel Rowlands, *The letting of humours blood in the head-vaine*
Fritdtjof Nansen, *The structure and combination*

of the historical elements of the central nervous system
Gerard Legh, *The accedens of armory*
Robert Boyle, *The experimental history of colours*
James Wilson, *Biography of the blind*
Robert Tailor, *The hogge hath lost his pearle*
William Prynne, *A gagge for long-hair'd rattle-heads*
Whistle-Binkie

Nothing drew my particular notice until I discovered a three-volume novel by Berthold Auerbach, the nineteenth-century regionalist; the title was quite unknown to me. Opening it at random, I came across a chapter whose heading was "The Otiose Creator"; and my chance reading† of it gave me the first clue to the solution of the enigmas that lay between me and Mr. Wayl's heritage.

† The original text has been published as an Appendix to this work.

“THE OTIOSE CREATOR”

Gottlieb told Maria his dream of the previous night.

“In a gray silence I floated upwards through the sky, past the clouds, past the stars. Then I came to another world and thought, ‘This surely is Paradise.’ At first I crossed meadows, then wooded hills with pretty streams. Beyond them was the city, extensive but surprisingly quiet.

“I walked down from the hills to enter the city, but I had not so much as reached the outskirts when I was stopped by a pitiful sight. A man lay in the ditch by the path I had taken. I have never seen anyone so thin: through his rags one could see, all over his body, the points of bones about to pierce the skin; and the skin, gray and transparent like greasy parchment, had indeed begun to break and flake off in many places. Little wheezing groans issued from his throat, wringing my heart in spite of horror and disgust. I ran towards the city to find someone to help me succor this poor creature. Barely arrived at the first buildings, I came upon a policeman whom I summoned to follow me. We were soon at the side of the helpless wretch. But when the latter saw who was with me, he loosed a shriek of horror, then became so still I thought he no longer breathed. As for the policeman, he had at first seemed indifferent to the prostrate man; but after the shriek he approached him, raised his club and struck him a terrible blow on the temple. Then the policeman saluted and started back towards the city. I sat there for a while in a shocked daze. After a while I looked at the stricken man, and I shuddered at the appearance of his head: the blow had truly bashed the skull in, making an indentation from eyebrow to crown of brownish-blue. Yet as I looked the eyes opened, and the wheezing groans started again, sharper than before. Then the eyes turned on me—or rather one of them turned, for the other had been immobilized in its socket by the blow—the eye turned on me, the groaning stopped, and the stricken man fell as silent as he had in front of the policeman. Incredulous, I turned towards the city.

"At the place where I had found the policeman another man now stood, as if waiting for me, and I soon recognized our nephew young Hans, who had died while at the university in Freiburg.

" 'Uncle Gottlieb!' he cried when he had made me out. 'Welcome, welcome! I didn't know it was you, but I should have—always the model of civic duty. Confidentially, though, I think I should tell you—of course this is not to be taken as criticism, what you did was perfectly all right—I should tell you that outside the city they are allowed to do pretty much what they want. I see that you protest—it was in truth a fearful noise he made, but wasn't that after you had called the angel? You see, I watched the whole business, and it seemed to me that that fellow was behaving himself—considering the fact of course that he was outside the city. He wasn't really making very much noise and he was well concealed by the ditch. Naturally you did come upon him unexpectedly and it must have been a nasty shock—but you should see the ones farther out, especially up in the mountains: nauseating! And you should hear *them* scream. I had to go there only last month to gather some hair (it's amazing how hair grows on them no matter how abominable their condition), and I could swallow nothing but biscuits and milk for days. We should be grateful for the present policy, even if it is rather easy on them and deprives the rest of us of the consolation of witnessing their state.'

" 'Then they are the damned?' I asked.

" 'What a funny thing to say, Uncle Gottlieb!—although they must surely feel like the damned,' Hans answered with a laugh. 'No, it is better that they be left free in the country to lie in the open and lament than that they be kept in town and there stuffed in subcellars and publicly beaten. For no matter how thoroughly they are muffled and no matter how much pain is inflicted on them, it seems that the necessary municipal silence can never be attained: not only are they too miserable, they are simply too numerous. Imagine: 190,000,000,000 at the last census. Furthermore the space they occupied has been redeemed and converted into dormitories for the laborers that are really very cozy (cozy enough for them at any rate). —But tell me, Uncle: how long has it been since you arrived?'

" 'I was coming to the city for the first time when I found that man in the ditch.'

" 'Then you've just arrived? Good Lord, come over here, out of sight. Oh Uncle, why didn't you tell me? Thank goodness you've got your Sunday clothes on: ah, that's a stroke of luck—you could not imagine how sensitive they are to such things. Formerly, it seems, when the press of entrants was not so great, there was more tolerance as to such details; but nowadays one's respectability is established by one's shoes! Oh Uncle, I am happy for you—you can be certain they will listen to you, and you will have a chance to tell them about your farm and your livestock and your savings so carefully amassed (you may thank yourself for that trouble, Uncle!), and then you will be safe. Now you must not expect too much—you will have to work a little, probably in the aerial farms, but you will have all the farm hands you want to help you; and with your savings you should be granted a satisfactory life. You will then be able to prepare the way for Aunt Maria—influence is always a help, although of course yours will be small. But that can wait: the thing to do now is to get you registered. I'm afraid it may take rather a long while, but at least you'll know once it's over that you are established *forever*. Believe me, that's a relief such as you've never experienced, and never will again.'

"Hans took me by the arm and led me towards the center of the city.

" 'Now let me remind you,' he said, 'to be careful in telling about your possessions. Don't mention everything (don't tell them how many hens you have, Uncle!)—just be sure not to leave out any major item. You see, while money isn't the only thing that counts —an influential protector can redeem individuals without a penny—it is frequently decisive in determining the category into which the new arrival is directed.'

" 'But shouldn't I first point to other signs of worth?' I asked. 'The love I have borne my family, the care . . .'

" 'Yes, yes, Uncle, but they know of those things already. And then they really make so little difference. Such behavior is of course admired and welcomed, but it is very hard to evaluate. It is also so common—how few there are who cannot find excuses for their misbehavior! and in this respect kindness is the rule here—so common that it is useless as a basis for the complex classification our administrative angels have to make. Thus other elements are considered—among them wealth. (You understand that there is no money here, heaven forbid! One is supplied according to one's classification.) You may reasonably ask, isn't the good life of a poor man more meritorious than the same life lived by someone richer? But in this matter, the truth seems to be that the advantages of money not only should, but do, permit the rich to live superior moral lives. It appears that the poorer one is, the less time and energy one has for those beneficial actions that the comfortable are able to perform practically as a matter of course. So you see, taking money into consideration when establishing a person's dossier is anything but an injustice. It is really a question of giving people what they deserve, and this means what they are capable of, which in turn is decided by what they have been. Should a half-starved savage who has lived his life like an animal be given the same rewards as a man—for instance, an administrator or a poet—who has shown himself capable of service of a higher order? That would hardly be justice.'

"I walked on, clinging to Hans's arm in a state of bewilderment. We walked through many clean streets, and as we neared the center, the streets became grand avenues planted with sycamores, paved with tiles of many-colored moss.

" 'Hans, tell me: is the Good Lord here?'

"Indicating the splendid avenue before us he answered, 'How can you doubt it?'

" 'Does he know of such things as the man in the ditch?'

" 'Oh Uncle, heaven forbid! The poor Dear has already endured enough; and He has made all this possible for us. What ingratitude if we did not ensure Him peace at last! He has given *us* that, and more. He no longer must spend His Hours on the care of His Kingdom, but lives withdrawn in the most magnificent of palaces set in the fairest of parks, attended by those who best know His wants—His ministering angels are the highest classification of heaven. He lives in bliss, surrounded as He is only with praise and adoration; and His happiness is our sweetest joy (Uncle, forgive my tears!). But look smart now! Here are the registration bureaux.'

"We had come to a gray building of many storeys, as vast as a fortress. There were two lines of people in front of it, one of those entering, the other of those leaving. As we approached, the latter was interrupted by a group that bustled down the great steps. Two uniformed men held a woman between them and hurried her along. The skin below her mouth was covered with a purple cancer. She disappeared with her guards down a nearby sidestreet that I had not noticed. Many such groups were proceeding down it.

" 'She is being taken out of the city,' Hans remarked.

" 'Like the man I found this morning?'

" 'Yes. Disease is not allowed in the city either, unless it is completely benign.'

" 'But surely the doctors here . . .'

" 'Oh, the doctors have all retired comfortably. It's their due, don't you think? Not quite all, as a matter of fact—there are a few so obsessed with disease that they have given up their greater privileges to live with the sick. They are thought to be a little crazy—can you imagine making such a choice for eternity?'

" 'Then that woman's disease will go on untreated?'

" 'Very likely.'

" 'But it will get no worse?'

" 'If its natural course is to get worse, it will.'

" 'But then sooner or later the disease will kill her.'

" 'No, no: no matter what happens, she will not die.'

"We had reached the top of the steps and were about to enter the building. All at once such a feeling of horror came over me that I cried out and, trembling, woke up. But once awake I realized, Maria, what had given me that feeling of horror. It was not horror at the vision before me, but at the thought that I too might be 'taken out of the city.' And the relief that followed was not only relief at waking but that of knowing that even *there* I had nothing to fear, and I thanked God in my heart for giving me the good things of this world.

"I remember that as I passed from sleep to waking I turned towards Hans, who smiled as he receded in my sight, and cried: 'Then it is only the same?' and he answered, 'The same, Uncle, but forever: world without end!'

"O Maria, hail to the Johnstones! the bloody Johnstones! the fucking Johnstones! the enemies of things as they are! They have come back to their own, they have come back to Alba as kings. May their Gypsy girl have wicked teeth in her cunt!"

THE CUSTOMS HOUSE (II)

No sooner had I finished the chapter than a voice behind me said: I regret, sir—and turning I saw, next to the official who had first spoken to me, a small man dressed all in green (tweed, shirting, silk and suede)—that it will be impossible for me to give you the information you need.

Are you the director here? I asked. Perhaps then you might help me out with another problem, if you can spare me a few minutes.

I showed him the concluding paragraph of "The Otiose Creator." Can you tell me who these Johnstones are?

Oh dear! However did you find *that?* Well: you see there is a family in this town called Johnstone (quite the *gratin*), but these are others—indeed the Earl no doubt suppressed Auerbach's book out of consideration for the proper Johnstones. The "Johnstones" Auerbach refers to are the family of a disowned bastard son of one of the Earls of Mar. This son came here around 1780 (from the colonies, I believe), making all kinds of trouble, taking the name of Johnstone, and pretending of all things to be not only of noble but of royal blood—I suppose that's why Auerbach says the Johnstones *sind als Königen nach Alba heimgekehrt.* He even adopted a coat of arms—a stupid pretension when everyone knew he had no claim to any title whatsoever.

Could you describe the coat of arms?

No, but I'll look it up for you if you like. (I'm awfully sorry I can't help you out about that adze.) It's surely listed in Cremlin-Bicêtre; let's see—Jargon, Jessel, Jinemevicz, Job: here we are, *Johnstone:*

Gold a bend silver with halberd gules

and the reason above:

L'herminette à la taille du roy!

There!

A loonlike factory whistle resounded from the foggy air outside while I studied the heraldic register.

After a long moment the green director began looking at me with diffidence; so I thanked him and—once he had sternly told me that the customs house contained no other documents on the "Johnstones"—went out.

The director accompanied me to the door.

You were fortunate, he said, to have heard our madrigal this morning—strange to say, our apparatus works in indirect proportion to the fineness of the weather: it needs a truly foul day to hear the music fair.

"HIS PRISM AND SILENT FACE"

To me, that day was anything but foul.

L'herminette à la taille du roy! Kingfitted ermine; or a kingsized adze. The halberd in the coat of arms, a plain bill, was an image of my "adze": *l'herminette* could mean only it.

Then was not the first doubly-pretending Johnstone the stone-not-king of the riddle? I felt sure of it, and sure that I should find proof in Alva.

I remembered how, during the race at Mr. Wayl's,

the adze had appeared first red amid white light, and later, under the charm of "Midas's finger," red in a haze of gold. These were the very colors of the heraldic shield.

After lunch I went to the Alva town hall and approached a clerk with the request to examine certain municipal records.

The odd Johnstones? he asked. Ah, the best of the lot lived long after that time—that was poor Inno Johnstone, who died forty-some years ago, poor unlucky man he was. Let me tell you about him; he deserves his bit of fame. After that you can look up any part of the family you damn well please!

The last of his family, Innocent Johnstone had, I learned, lived a short strange life. Showing early an exceptional interest in physical science, he had for two years been a brilliant student at St. Andrew's, whence he had been sent down for disciplinary reasons. He had pursued his scientific studies independently, living alone, devoting all his immense inheritance to the construction of experimental equipment.

In those days much research was being done in the effects of extreme heat and cold, and Johnstone naturally shared the interest of the scientific world. His own interest became an enthusiasm when, almost by accident, he made the first of his extraordinary discoveries.

In the Silver Glen of Alva there was to be found, diffused in the water of certain pools, a crystalline substance popularly known as fleshmetal. It existed only in minute quantities and was hardly known outside the town—and even there many, having never seen it, thought its existence to be legendary. The substance was remarkable in that it destroyed solid materials upon touching them; many of those who had tried to handle it had been maimed, and none had succeeded in bringing any of it away. Johnstone found that fleshmetal responded to magnetic influence, and he solved the problem of transporting it by constructing magnetized "trays" whose current, strong enough to draw up the dangerous particles, was too weak to bring them into direct contact: the fleshmetal was carried suspended (either in water or air) at a fraction of a millimeter beneath the tray.

Once he had secured a small stock of fleshmetal, Johnstone submitted it to numerous tests. He was unable to reduce the substance to component elements. Its violent corrosiveness was, he discovered, the result of abnormally vigorous molecular motion, untypical of any other known solid; but he was unable to explain this phenomenon in any way until he decided to observe the influence of low temperatures on fleshmetal. He had prepared his apparatus—airpump and baths of liquid air—to reach temperatures well below freezing. To his surprise, he had hardly started the experiment when the suspended particles under observation disappeared. Repeating the steps taken, he determined that solid fleshmetal became a gas when cooled to −2° C.

Many a scientist might have then announced his discovery to the world. But Johnstone was too absorbed in his research to think of giving it up.

High temperatures (necessarily limited by the melting-points of the metals composing the magnetic tray) brought about an increase in fleshmetal's molecular activity, but no sign of a change of state, either to liquid or gas. The scientist resumed his experimentation with low temperatures. To begin with he succeeded, using baths of liquid oxygen together with a mercurial vacuum, in reducing gaseous fleshmetal to a temperature (—198° C) at which its molecular motion was so calmed as to render it innocuous and easier to handle. But his further efforts, aimed at liquefaction, were vain. Even the use of liquid helium, as a last step in the "cascade method," with prolonged heatless expansion of gaseous fleshmetal, failed. Not, however, entirely: Johnstone observed, towards the end of his final attempt, certain faint white drops on the innermost wall of his apparatus, and it was possible, he thought, that these marked a beginning of liquefaction. The temperature at that moment was no higher than —269° C, probably even a degree lower: that is, only three degrees above absolute zero. Could greater cold be produced?

Johnstone did not know what to do next. He was tantalized by the white drops, and yet he knew that he had exhausted the known resources of physics. Since he had already spent a great part of his considerable fortune, he considered the possibility of abandoning. Then his good luck saved him.

One morning, while his Irish maid swept out his laboratory, Johnstone was examining certain ordinary materials at his spectroscope in order to check the instrument. He was engaged in observing some iodine, heated to 700° C in a cyanite dish, when an inexplicable line of bright cupric green appeared in the spectrum. It vanished presently, returned briefly, again disappeared. After a moment Johnstone noticed that the appearance of the green line seemed to correspond to the more prolonged proximities of his biddy. The following conversation, reported by the scientist to the town clerk's father, then took place:

Agnes, come here, please!

Oh sirr!

Agnes . . . ?

Ah Mr. Inno, forgive me! It's them mumbleberries I et in the woods laast evenin.

What? Eat mumbleberries?

Indeed, sirr, they're me favorite pickin: but they do make a bawdy faart.

(The clerk interrupted his narrative to inform me that the name *mumbleberry* came not from the caramel stickiness of the berries, which sometimes impeded clear speech, but from a rash on the legs, supposedly brought on by the fruit, called *mormal:* the original name was *mormalberry*.)

Thus Inno Johnstone made his second great discovery. A new inert gas was soon isolated and its existence spectroscopically confirmed by electrical examination in Plücker tubes. Johnstone found the gas in a pure state, as clusters of tiny bubbles, in the soft concavity of the mumbleberry where the stem enters the fruit. The name he chose for the gas was *anagnon*, referring both to his biddy's name and the "unchaste" way she had brought it to his attention.

Johnstone must have felt that angels were helping him when he learned, testing the new gas for its properties, that it could not be liquefied under exhausted helium; for this signified that anagnon had a critical temperature lower than that of any known gas and so might serve to liquefy fleshmetal. It did in fact: by expanding gaseous fleshmetal under exhausted anagnon, Inno obtained liquid fleshmetal at a temperature he estimated as −272° C (1° Abs).

He was still unsatisfied: for this last experiment had left perplexing questions unanswered. How was it possible that at one degree above absolute zero fleshmetal could show no tendency to solidify, and anagnon itself no sign of liquefaction? In theory all matter should attain a solid state before reaching the point of ultimate cold. The margin of one degree seemed improbably small to allow the final transformations of the two new elements. (For fleshmetal, he had decided, was also an unknown element.) Was anagnon a uniquely irreducible gas? Or fleshmetal an irreducible liquid? What alternative could there be?

Johnstone decided that the most reasonable course was to try to solidify fleshmetal. Again he liquefied a quantity of fleshmetal (this procedure took two weeks) and prolonged the methods of the experiment, drawing off expanding anagnon from its case of solid helium. As the vacuum thus created increased, he agitated the liquid fleshmetal in order to promote that molecular regrouping that would begin solidification. After eleven weeks of painstaking work, Johnstone saw solid crystals form—only a first few, and only briefly, for in a moment his apparatus disintegrated.

The town clerk recalled the day of the catastrophe, a pleasant day in mid-August, with all Alva still. The clerk, then a boy of eight, was playing in his yard when he heard a sinister roar. Going into the street he beheld Inno Johnstone's house sprouting with enormous clublike branches of snow that projected through every door, window and chimney to a distance of more than thirty feet. In a very short time these white limbs dissolved "into thin air."

Johnstone had miraculously survived. The wreck of his equipment, brought on by the virtually absolute vacuum he had created, had thrown him to the ground. He had lain insensible while the released cold froze the air in wild columns that surged over him towards the apertures of room and house, leaving him unscathed. Revived, his first concern had been for the harm the scattered fleshmetal might have done when, cast into the air, it had returned to its original state. Fortunately all of it had fallen on the ground, its infinitesimal bits thereupon burning their way into the earth. (The largest hole thus made, about a quarter of an inch across, was sounded to a depth of eighty-two feet, at which point water was touched.)

Prudence, the advice of friends and the orders of the town council would have obliged Johnstone to leave off. Instead he moved to an isolated farm and invested in new equipment all that remained of his fortune. (Each pound of liquefied helium cost him three thousand guineas.)

He was haunted now by a single vision: fleshmetal crystallized at a temperature he dared not name. Only seen for an instant, the crystals had existed. Unlike the crystalline fleshmetal of the Silver Glen, they had not destroyed the materials they had touched. Was this because the extreme cold had rendered them harmless as it had the liquid and the colder gaseous fleshmetal?

Extreme cold? The anagnon had remained pure gas; the vacuum had been absolute. What had the temperature been?

Was there no limit of cold?

Johnstone, half admitting the hypothesis his imagination had caught on, assumed, "to get on with the job," that beyond absolute zero temperature might exist. He began preparing for his last experiment.

He constructed in his new apparatus a device that would, when the crystals of fleshmetal appeared, automatically reduce the vacuum that had nearly destroyed him; as well as numerous systems for observing and controlling whatever temperature might occur at crystallization.

The two years of preparation saw Johnstone so neglect his health that he was an ill man when the experiment started. Yet his last sick days were happy.

Fleshmetal crystals again appeared, at a temperature of "—x° Abs." Their crystallization was accompanied by a transformation of molecular activity from a standstill, at .01° Abs, to violent motion, suggestive of heat. Other substances, cooled with solid fleshmetal and anagnon, underwent a similar transformation. Johnstone realized that beyond absolute zero a strange "heat" obtained, which he called *infraheat.*

To investigate it, he built an infracaloric space enclosed in a vacuum jacket, itself encased in solid helium. There, combining in an atmosphere of anagnon various materials cooled below 0°Abs, he created a wide range of infracaloric temperatures, measured with a water thermometer on whose scale + 1° Inf = —1° Abs.

In infraheat, the peculiarities fleshmetal had shown at normal temperatures were common to all matter. 0° was the "hot" limit of infraheat, at which molecular activity was greatest, while it declined as the degrees of the Infra scale rose. Nevertheless, with this lessening of infraheat the state of matter changed as if "normal" heat were increased, so that solids became liquids, liquids gases, and gases solid.

As the changes of fleshmetal above 0°Abs had implied, the cycle of matter was thus seemingly infinite. The destructive power of fleshmetal itself was evidently a corollary to the extension of its infracaloric properties into the realm of normal heat; for in infraheat it lacked such power.

Water was the only exception to the reversal of changes that appeared with infraheat: at 1°Inf it was vapor, becoming a boiling liquid at 175° Inf and ice at 278°Inf. It was consequently well adapted, its properties in infraheat being known, to serve as the fluid in Johnstone's thermometer.

Johnstone had planned to explore the relationship between the three exceptional substances, water, fleshmetal and anagnon; but he was not given enough time to do so. His last work concerned the mechanical questions raised in a world where iron softened with cold, where mercury hardened with heat, and where, between the boiling- and freezing-points of water, wood was a liquid and diamonds a light gas. Before dying he achieved infracaloric combustion, burning molten salt in glass air. He had hoped to build machines for his new world before succumbing; and his last words concerned an airplane entirely of butter.

Johnstone had contracted a rash of blains on his legs, brought on, in confirmation of popular legend, by the excessive amounts of mumbleberries he handled in maintaining his supply of anagnon. The sores having become infected, Johnstone's worn health yielded fast. He died at the age of thirty-four, without putting his extraordinary findings in coherent form. At his own request his laboratory, abandoned in operation, was destroyed by shelling while he was still on his deathbed, so that no one should be harmed by another, possibly more dangerous disintegration of his equipment. His few admirers, of whom the clerk's father was one, had tried to interest the scientific world in the work they had long followed (if only half comprehendingly). But unluckily a drought parched the pools of the Silver Glen, and all their fleshmetal vanished, the name soon after resuming the reputation it had long borne as an excrescence of folkish fancy.

ABE JOHNSTONE'S LETTER

When the clerk had finished his story, he showed me into the town library where he gave me access to the regional archives. An hour's patience brought forth the records of the first false Johnstone; among them I found a curious document.

Its bulk comprised a letter evidently addressed to a number of newspapers and reviews of the day. Pinned to the first of its sheets were four slips of paper inscribed with inks of differing colors. The topmost of these slips read in faint pink ink:

Pennsylvania Gazette, Independant Reflector
Keimer's Gazette (Barbados)
Mémoires Secrètes de la République des Lettres
General Advertiser, Grub Street Journal, Fog's Journal, Reid's Journal, Mist's Journal, Oedipus or the Postrian Remounted, History of the Works of the Learned:

Rejected.

The second slip, in purple ink, was as follows:

Evening Salem Gazette, N.Y. Gazetteer, A's & B's, Royal American Magazine, Turtle Bay Reflector & Oyster Bay Mirror
Keimer's Gazette (Barbados)
La Vespa Veronese, Il Caffè
Trudolyubivary Ptchelà
Le Radoteur, La Queue de l'Abeille, L'Armée Littéraire, Nécrologe des Hommes Célèbres de France
Public Advertiser, Public Ledger, St. James's Chronicle, Cock's Chronicle, The Rambler, The Bee, The Connoisseur, The Voluptuary, The Looker-on:

Rejected.

The third slip, slightly larger than the others, was in black ink:

The Mass. Sentinel & The Republican Journal, Cheshire Republican, Green Mountain Postboy, Con. Courant, Sodus Social Register, Franklin Repository, Maryland Inland & Baltimore Advertiser, Minerva Advertiser, Adler,

Paine's Labour, Rivington's N.Y. Loyal Gazette, Mathews' Universal Asylum
Colon's Intelligencer (Quebec)
Asiatick Miscellany
Gaceta de Madrid
Mercure de Suède
Mémoires de Bachaumont, L'Observateur Observé, Journal de Verdun
Public Advertiser, Morning Chronicle, Thersites, Times, English Magazine, Monstrous Magazine, Pandora's Box (A Magazine for Gentlewomen), Sauce for the Gander, Macaroni Magazine, European Magazine, A New Review, British Critic, The Lounger, Potter & Poet:

Rejected.

The last slip, whose brief list was of a blackish chocolate tone difficult to define, read thus:

American Museum of the Dead
Galeria di Venere
Nouvelle Bibliothèque Ecossaise, Le Croulant
The Ash & the Wren, A Pathetic Magazine.

(Rejected)

By looking up the dates of the periodicals listed, I reckoned that Johnstone had first sent out his hapless letter around 1745 and had not abandoned his attempts to publish it until 1803.

This was the letter's text:

Sir,

To the east of the Scots burgh of Alva in the county of Clackmannanshire, a pleasant valley, through which the waters of a cascade flow with a quick and rejoicing course, bears the denomination of Silver Glen. The epithet of *silver* is thought to be expressive of those riches that once abounded in its earth, to which abandoned workings yet bear supposed witness. But the name of this celebrated spot is a testimony of religion, not a record of commerce.

During their long servitude under the Imperial and Barbarian yoke, the native and foreign tribes of Italy had mutually adopted and corrupted each other's superstitions. The Christians, indeed, practised the worship of Christ; but they disgraced and polluted it with a various mixture of pagan idolatry. Others revered the memory of Sylvius, the ancient prophet and king of the Romans; yet the obsolete and mysterious language of his cult opened a field of dispute to numberless sects, who variously explained the fundamental doctrines of their religion, and were all indifferently derided by those who rejected the divine mission and miracles of the king. To escape the idolaters, the schismatics, and the unbelievers, a pious Roman, who had taken the sacred name of Sylvius, summoned his followers from all the corners of Italy. These disciples, who had so long sighed in contempt and obscurity, obeyed the welcome summons; and on the appointed day, in the first years of the fourteenth century, appeared to the number of about seven thousand. The hasty assembly gradually coalesced into a great and permanent society.

Under the guidance of Sylvius and his successors, they wandered over Europe in search of a place where they might establish and pursue the practice of the religion that united them. A century later, after many discouragements, they finally found refuge in Scotland on the lands of Alexander Stewart, the Earl of Mar, whom they had converted to their faith: and by him they were granted, in frank almoign, for the construction of their shrines, a fair valley which they named the Glen of Sylvius. Such was, and indeed is, the proper appellation of the place, which only took the name of Silver's Glen, and later Silver Glen, through the long corruptions of usage.

This good fortune of the wise and peaceable followers of Sylvius endured for over a century before it was at last succeeded by the most terrible calamity. Covetousness and prejudice finally concurred in representing the Sylvians as a society of atheists, who, by the most daring refusal of the beliefs of the age, had merited the severest animadversion of the civil magistrate. The counsels of princes are more frequently influenced by views of temporal advantage than by consideration of abstract and speculative truth. A prudent magistrate might have observed with pleasure the progress of a religion which diffused among the people a pure, benevolent and universal system of ethics, adapted to every duty and every condition of life. But the mysteries of the Sylvian faith and worship were concealed from the eyes of strangers, and even of catechumens, with a secrecy which served to excite their wonder and animosity; the pious solitariness of the Sylvians made their conduct, or perhaps their designs, appear in a much more serious and criminal light, inspiring the multitude with the apprehension of some danger which would arise from the new sect. It may be that the rulers of the land shared these fears or at the least resented the holy title of King which the Sylvian chiefs assumed. But I may say with certainty that it was rather the parsimony or poverty of the family of Mar that compelled them to deviate from the rule of conduct which had deserved the love and confidence of the Sylvians, whose reputed wealth finally served only to attract a bold and barbarous rapaciousness. The Earl of Mar dexterously persuaded the Scots king of the seditious hostility of the innocent sect, and in the year 1546, under the authority of the crown, and with the agency of a fanatical populace, the Earl reaped the harvest of his malevolence. In a tumult of cruelty and indignation, the habitations of the Sylvians were pillaged, their sanctuary ravaged by a promiscuous crowd of Gypsies and Beggars, and they themselves slaughtered by the soldiery of the Earl, who seized their goods and moneys in the name of royal justice. Four thousand persons are said to have perished in the massacre. The survivors, numbering about five hundred, mostly natives of the country converted to Sylvian beliefs, were threatened with death, unless they swore an oath of fidelity or went into perpetual exile; but rejecting such alternatives, they broke away before their punishment could be inflicted, and withdrew into the natural haven of the Ochils.

Three centuries of persecution reduced somewhat the descendants of these survivors. Yet so sensible were the Sylvians of the imperfection of religion without communal practice, that, in all this time, the name of Sylvius has been borne without interruption by their leaders, and nobly borne. The religious exercise of the united sect has been for these chiefs the important and unremitting object of their lives; nor was time and place allowed to excuse them for forgetting their temporal rights over Sylvius's Glen. These holy Kings have been chosen by tradition, because of the bastardy of Alexander Stewart, from the bastard and outcast issue of the Earls of Mar; the exercise of their sacred functions has required of them an immaculate purity both of mind and of body; it is incumbent on them to excel in decency and virtue the rest of their fellow-citizens. Their authority has been recognized from time to time by men of particular genius: thus Rolando Lasso, the prince of musicians and the familiar of kings, prophesied that the bastard-born Sylvius should return to rule anew.

The time is at hand for that prophecy to be fulfilled, and the last of the Sylvian leaders, the author of this letter, has indeed returned to

Alva. Yet the behaviour of the present Earl of Mar appears to be as reprehensible as that of his predecessors. In my general view of the persecution first authorized in the year 1541 and which thereafter continued unabated, I have purposely refrained from describing the sufferings and deaths of Sylvian martyrs. It would be an easy task from ancient acts to collect a long series of horrid and disgusting pictures, and to fill many pages with all the varieties of torture which savage executioners could inflict on the human body. But there is more propriety in declaring a less pathetic, but no less appalling fact, namely, that the Earls of Mar have held and continue to hold against justice and humanity the rightful property of innocent men. The injustice of their possession is apparent in the unnatural measures they have taken to preserve it: for not only did the Earls who succeeded their first criminal exemplar obstruct the Sylvians by force and cruelty, but to secure for themselves the sacred glen, they had it scooped into a prodigious but *imaginary* mine; precious metals were artificially introduced as props to their consummate pretence; and although the pretended workings and issue soon disappeared, the defences raised to protect them remain a sinister and impenetrable barrier about the place.

These events, which heretofore have not been thought deserving of a place in history, have been productive of a memorable injustice, which has afflicted the disinherited of

Alva above three hundred years, and will be extinguished only with the presumption of the offenders. The inflexible zeal of liberty and devotion has animated the Sylvians to refuse obedience to the Usurpers, whose rights they dispute, and whose spiritual powers they deny. They have asserted with confidence, almost with exultation, that the rightful succession has been interrupted; that all the Earls of Mar have been infected by the contagion of greed and dishonesty; and that the prerogatives of lordship should be confined to the chosen portion of Sylvian believers, who alone have preserved inviolate the integrity of their faith and conduct.

Would that the family of Mar possessed one legitimate son whose genius and virtues might atone for the vice and folly of his fathers! Did such a one support this exalted faith, his name would deserve a place with Constantine, and his judgment would be justly entitled to all the applause philosophers might bestow upon it. But that motley gang, dictated by passion and by selfish motives, has disgraced useful and sublime truth with the most abject and dangerous persecution. Their ferocious sons, who disdain the salutary restraint of laws, are yet more anxious to preserve riches than to foster the religion of a society the object of their contempt and hatred; and their power is a stone of Tantalus, perpetually suspended over the peace and safety of a devoted sect. The measures which the present writer recommends are the dictates of a sincere and dedicated believer. I exhort the reader to strengthen the courage of our company with the example of noble solicitude; to attack the oppressor in his position and his property; to substitute, in the place of barbarian indifference, the sympathies of men interested in the defence of justice; to force, in such a moment of opportunity and danger, the quill from its shelf and the coin from its box; and to arm, for the protection of human right, the hands of earnest disciples.

The mischiefs that flow from the contests of ambition are usually confined to the times and places in which they have been agitated. But the religious discord of the friends and enemies of Sylvius has been renewed in every age and is yet maintained in the immortal hatred of the Earls of Mar. Our wonder is reasonably excited that they should presume to persevere in a privilege whose ancient presumptions they are incapable of defending honestly. But the feuds, the angers, and the protests of the Earls, are the feeble and pernicious efforts of old age, which exhaust the remains of strength and accelerate the decay of the powers of life.

In conclusion, let me express the hope that the condemnation of the wisest and most virtuous of sects will sufficiently offend the reason and humanity of the present age, that men may be roused to action, and justice be done at the last.

Your Faithful Servant,

ABENDLAND JOHNSTONE

Another paper was pinned beneath the signature. It was a note written in a strange hand, and its presence suggested that Johnstone had sent his letter to individuals as well as journals. The text was brief:

Rouen le 10 Brumaire An II

Monsieur,

Peut-être êtes-vous un bâtard, vous êtes sûrement un imposteur; car notre dernier roi est mort avant Louis de France. Je veille pour la Reine, que son règne soit éternel!

LA PLATIERE

Beneath these lines Johnstone had added:

—Alas! We are all dying.

"LA MESSE DE SIRE FADEVANT"

So it appeared that Abe Johnstone was the stone who was not a king—that La Platière qualified him an imposter confirmed my hunch. No doubt it would be prudent to complete my proof by finding out who La Platière was and by verifying the grounds on which he had condemned Johnstone. This promised to be anything but tedious work, for if I found La Platière's papers I should perhaps get other helpful information from them. The place where his note was written seemed the best point of departure for my inquiry, and I decided to go to Rouen at once.

I wanted before leaving Alva to visit "Sylvius's Glen." It lay east of the town a ways beyond the Customs House. I had hardly passed that dismal building when a rural policeman stopped me and directed me, on learning where I was headed, back to the town. He explained that he had orders (he did not say whose) to keep me out of the glen. Seeing my disappointment—he was a kindly-looking man, although enormous and rough, with flaming golden bangs—he consoled me with a description of the glen: aside from the waterfall, he said, it was a plain place, filled with stunted elms and overgrown with unkempt masses of traveler's joy. (I asked what this was; he defined it as a variety of clematis. I remarked that in my case it was singularly ill-named.)

Riding to Edinburgh I was bothered by an especially disturbing element of the muddled history I was investigating. Who was the queen that La Platière mentioned? Had she anything to do with Auerbach's Gypsy girl? When the Long Island Gypsy had explained the scenes of the adze to the novelist, he had called the woman there portrayed "our queen." Could the woman of the adze not be the saint Mr. Wayl had let me assume her to be? Yet Johnstone declared in his letter that "Gypsies and Beggars" had destroyed the Sylvian sanctuary, and made no reference to any queen or woman. To "provide a satisfactory explanation of the meaning" of the adze, as the will required, these inconsistencies would have to be resolved.

Examining the copy I had made of the letter to be certain I had missed no clue to this dilemma, I stopped short at the name of Rolando Lasso. I had become so absorbed in answering the first question of the will that I had practically forgotten the other two. If the renaissance composer figured in Johnstone's letter, there was a chance that information concerning *La Messe de Sire Fadevant* might lie with him—and hadn't I discovered King Johnstone through just such an unexpected slender reference?

I stayed over in Edinburgh to follow this bent. For two days I worked at the Advocates' Library without finding a hint that Lasso might in his life or work have had anything to do with the Sylvians, the Earls of Mar, or the adze; nor was any *Messe de Sire Fadevant* listed among his works, extant or not. As a last resort, I decided to check the most recent musicological reviews; and on the back cover of the current issue of *Neumata*, in the list of articles announced for future publication, I found this title:

Una Missa Fa Si Re, Opera Sconosciuta di Orlando di Lasso, di Prof. Annibale Bumbè (Siena)

I was overjoyed at my new luck. Nevertheless, I blamed myself for not recognizing the riddle within the second question of the will: the riddle being that *Sire Fadevant* signified *Fa devant Si Re*, and that consequently the mass was one composed on a theme whose opening notes were *fa, si* and *re*, and not one written by or for the Lord Fadevant whom I had hired two aspiring historians to track down.

I had planned to wait for the published article to learn more about the mass; but that very day a letter reached me with the news that Beatrice and Isidore

Fod were contesting Mr. Wayl's will. Convinced that the more evidence I could give the probate court, the safer my rights would be, I decided to visit Siena and elicit from Dr. Bumbè in person whatever he knew that might help me in my task.

AT THE PROFESSOR'S

On the evening of my second day in Siena, Professor Bumbè received me at his lodgings in the Palazzo Grembo-Maledetti. Once we were seated in his study, I explained the reason of my visit.

I shall tell you all I know in this matter, he said. Several years ago, a letter came to light that caused considerable interest in musicological circles. It had been written to the Flemish composer Lassus by his Parisian publisher Adrien Le Roy; its text was mainly an inquiry into the significance of a *Missa Fa Si Re* that the composer had written during his visit to the court of Charles IX in 1571. It was then common for musicians to write pieces on musical mottoes, and such works received their titles from the Guidonian note names of the motto. The unusual thing in this case was that Lassus had let it be known that the three notes of his motto—*fa, si* and *re*—were the abbreviations of secret Latin words.

As evidence of the public mystification that resulted, Le Roy lists some of the solutions he has heard proposed. Many thought that Lassus had simply paid tribute to the French king, who had received him handsomely; they advanced such phrases as

Faber sistrum Regis:
The composer is the king's sistrum

Court gossip produced interpretations less flattering to the royal family:

Fæx signat Reginam:
Rouge marks out the Queen

a reference to the aging Catherine de Médicis. The favorable effects on the king's impotence of his recent marriage to Elizabeth of Austria were invoked in

Favus sinus Reginae:
The Queen's lap is sweet as a honeycomb

and in

Fartor significat rectum:
The bird fattener portends uprightness

the idea of "bird" being a vulgar one, as in the German *Hahn* and your own "cock." Gossip likewise discovered references to current court peccadilloes:

Fabianus Sigismondo repuerascit:
For Sigismond, Fabian has become a boy again

or, concerning a supposed love affair of Lassus himself,

Faber Silviâ resupinâ:
The composer in the company of Silvia flat on her back

I mention in passing that since Lassus is etymologically a contraction of *là-dessus*, the last item shows a certain wit. The more literary hazarded such solutions as

Faber Sibylla Regorum:
The composer is the prophet of kings;
Facio sigla Regis:
I have made the abbreviation of a king

(this left the problem quite unsolved); and

Favillam Sibylla requirat:
The Sibyl searches for ashes,

perhaps a pedantic joke at would-be riddlers, perhaps a reference to Lassus's earlier *Prophetiae Sibyllarum.* Finally Le Roy jokingly imagines a possible reference to himself and concludes with two suggestions of his own:

Faber sine remuneratione:
Composer without pay

and

Fabrum siccat rex:
"Le Roy" is squeezing the composer dry

The letter ends with a plea for elucidation.

The only elucidation we have is not of the motto, but of another letter, long known but formerly not wholly explicable. This letter, written by Lassus to Le Roy, is surely an answer to the one I have described; for while it chiefly discusses royalties, one paragraph contains Lassus's comment on the *Missa Fa Si Re*. The paragraph begins by asking Le Roy if he has heard yet another interpretation of the motto—a dig at the lucrative business activity of Palestrina, then composer of the Sistine Chapel:

Fænus Sixtino remissio:
Dividends are his salvation

Lassus goes on to say that he has written a *chanson* on the motto of his mass; and that while there are three of Le Roy's proposed answers he cannot call false—*Facio sigla Regis, Faber Sibylla Regorum,* and (surprisingly) *Fæx signat Reginam*—yet these were not the three the music signified.

The very last words are interesting, implying that

the motto was discovered by those who listened to the mass—indeed, they would have had to be nearly tone-deaf not to notice the opening interval: for *fa-si* forms a tritone, condemned through the middle ages as the *diabolus in musica*. But the letter seemed to offer little hope of dispelling the mystery of the *Missa Fa Si Re*. For some time neither I nor anyone else got any farther with it. I suppose it was the irritating character of the problem that kept it in my mind despite the lack of progress. It was certainly irritating to have on the one hand such a tantalizing document as Le Roy's letter, and on the other hand only Lassus's stubborn half silence, without his mass,* and without either the text or the music of the *chanson* he mentions.

One day, however, I recalled a forgotten detail from my doctoral studies, thirty-odd years earlier. I then used to work in the British Museum preparing my thesis on Jacobean songbooks; and I had noticed once, in a 1616 collection of lyrics, an anonymous translation from the French that was remarkable in one respect. While the poem itself was a gloomy lover's complaint, its title was *Faisons Suzon*—words that might have been the opening of a light, "pastoral" French song. What possible connection did it have with the Lassus *chanson?* Only the slenderest one of the first two letters: Fa. But this, together with the inconsistency of title and text and a vague recollection of some typographical quaintness, was enough to have me write the museum asking for a photograph of the poem.

The museum's reply solved much of the enigma. A

* But see Appendix 2.

note accompanying the photostat informed me that the initial letter of each line was printed in red, and that red arabesques proceeded from these initials to encircle one or more of the letters following them. Here is a copy of the poem, with capitals standing for the initial letters and those within the arabesques.

I read:

FAithlesse thou art, my faith I giue to thee:
TEare out mine hart for hartlesse thou needst one,
OR take mine eies to see how blinde I bee.

SILVIa in thee my constancies vndone;
VMbre hath smircht my cheekes for thine too white
REGister of my soule, since thou hast none.

EMpresse of riuen soules the Queene of night
FAuoring mine anguish, to me sleeping came
TAbarded with thy sweets her serene might:

'Seest thou these cloakes that now beare *Siluias* name
REgalia of eies, smooth fleshe, and bright brocard,
TEXTures which patient Time hath giuen to Fame?

'FAme giuing owre to Ill-fame doth such discard,
VOyding the hing'd eie and the wouen gloue:
NIgardly patcht see Siluia slack'd and Mar'd.'

SIlent she doth, that thy cleere youth aproue
NIght-maring death, thee from thy beautie seuere:
STRAnge scull, that thou euen so my hart didst moue!

REuile me not! for I shal spurne thee neuere:
VOLatick Time shal turne, yet not my loue:
VIgil for thee I kept; and keepe, for euere.

Now, said the Professor, one must spell out the letters capitalized:

FATEORSILVIVMREGEMFATASRETEXTF
AVONISINISTRAREVOLVI

Next, one rewrites these letters, considering the syllables *fa*, *si* and *re* as the beginning of words:

FATEOR SILVIVM REGEM FATAS
RETEXT FAVONI SINISTRA REVOLVI

You will notice that whereas there are three *fa*'s and three *re*'s, there are only two *si*'s. The missing *si* is the S of "seest" in line ten. It stands for Silvius, as it did at first, and so does not need to be fully spelled. (The italicization of *Siluias* farther on in the same line removes any doubt as to its meaning.) Taking this into account we have:

FATEOR SILVIVM REGEM FATA SIL-
VIVM RETEXT FAVONI SINISTRA RE-
VOLVI

All that remains to be done is to fill out the shortened words. RETEXT must be *retexunt*, and the last three words make best sense as *Favonius sinistrâ revolvit.* Here then is the secret message in its final threefold form:

Fateor Silvium Regem:
I acknowledge Silvius as king

Fata Silvium retexunt:
either The Fates undo Silvius
or The Fates weave Silvius anew

Favonius sinistrâ revolvit:
The west wind returns on the left

In asking the British Museum for that song I had hit the mark. The verses luckily remembered from years before were without doubt a translation from the text of Lassus's *chanson*—or rather not a translation but a new poem that transcribed the secret letters of the original, the sign of their presence lying in the French title, kept for the English text. It becomes clear that in referring Le Roy to this *chanson* Lassus was answering his question honestly. I would say that the presence of the motto in the mass served merely to draw attention to the *chanson* (what better opportunity than a royal mass?) and that Lassus was telling the truth when he refused to disown three of the solutions that Le Roy has reported:

I have made the abbreviation of a king
The composer is the prophet of kings
Red (if not rouge) marks out the queen

But why "queen"? Why didn't Lassus in his letter correct *reginam* to *regem,* as the poem's secret sense demands? That I haven't found out; nor do I know who Silvius might be—perhaps a current allegorical name for some pretender, or for Henri III himself? There is no evidence for such a hypothesis. And I cannot explain the second and third sentences.

When I suggested that *sinistrâ* might indicate bastardy, Dr. Bumbè cut me short.

That possibility occurred to me—Charles IX had a natural son; but Charles of Angoulême? As for the queen, perhaps she was no queen but simply Regina Wäckinger. Who will ever know, or care? I leave spurious conjecture to Le Roy.

The professor had crossed his study and seated himself at an upright piano. Drawing a small square of sandpaper from his waistcoat pocket, he began methodically sanding the white keys of the instrument.

I cannot stand to have them shiny, he explained. If my fingers slip I break into a cold sweat. Even so, I play little—the count detests music.

He brought both hands down on a full C-major chord. But the depressed keys produced no sound except for the click of his nails on their roughened ivory backs.

FELIX NAMQUE

Midnight struck while I was returning to my hotel. As I followed the dark and sinuous slope of the Via Grover-Whalen, I reflected on the recent interview.

Lasso's cryptic sentences were plain. The unraveling and reweaving of Sylvius—surely Silvius was he, and surely the double meaning of *Fata Silvium retexunt* was intentional—signified an unbroken royal succession. Favonius returning meant that as the west wind of spring renewed the life of the fields, each bastard king brought prosperity with him. That the *diabolus in musica* was the signal of Lasso's message implied that this was, as the later Earls of Mar had evidently claimed, heretical; and the coded transmission of the message pointed to a widespread conspiracy of the sect. Once again the queen had appeared, mysteriously as ever in Lasso's third hint, more tangibly in the fervent text of the poem. What was the truth of the adze's engraved story?

I had a sure answer to the second question of the will, and a probable answer to the first. I had to confirm the latter, and pursue my investigations in the hope that I might come across a clue to the nature of the "Old Man's Beard."

The next day I set out for France, reaching Rouen in forty-eight hours. It was easy enough to identify La Platière, who to my surprise turned out to be the celebrated Girondist, Jean-Marie Roland de la Platière; but the records of the statesman, like those of Lasso, showed no sign of a connection with the Sylvians. I pursued my inquiries in the archives of every town where Roland had lived: Nantes, Thizy-Ouzoult, Lyons, Amiens, and finally Paris. In none did I find a useful fact, and at last, every public record examined, I sought out Roland's descendants. There was only one of them left in France, but I discovered him easily, for he was a celebrity in his own right, and a man whom I should have been curious to meet in ordinary circumstances.

He was M. Félix Namque, a painter settled in Paris, whose fame had grown so rapidly during the preceding decade that he was established at the age of thirty-five as a leader of postwar art. His merited vogue had followed the notoriety given his unique style of coloring. In each of his pictures the colors were never equivalent to those of their subject—they were always highly "interpreted." Yet they did not seem to be the mere result of fancy, taste or any personal predilection; they rather gave the impression of following some systematic distortion. Critics and amateurs had exchanged numberless fatuities trying to reveal the principle governing M. Namque's methods, but none of their suppositions and analyses, no matter how ingenious or thorough, could completely account for the coloring of even a single picture; and explaining the ensemble of the artist's work seemed a goal quite out of sight.

I had written to M. Namque frankly describing my plight. His quick answer invited me in the kindest terms to call on him at his studio, located on the top floor of the foamrubber building of the rue Ostende, in Passy. At the time of my visits he was engaged in finishing the portrait of Alut Andreori, the young Basque torero who was the latest star of the bullfighting world. Andreori was known in Spain as El Porrón because of his winedark complexion (a birthmark covered his whole head) and because his nose stuck up in a long thin cone, like the spout of a Spanish wineflask. I had heard that El Porrón was an example of skill, courage and dignity such as had never been seen in the bullring. He worked so close to the bull that several of his admirers of both sexes had received from the acuteness of their empathy various stigmata-like wounds—rents of pathetic reality in their thighs, abdomens and chests, according to the passage of the horn. El Porrón himself had never been seriously hurt, and he was suspected by the credulous of hiring witches to transfer his gorings to his more sensitive fans. It was practically miraculous that he was still alive. M. Namque was painting the bullfighter dressed for the ring, wearing in his pigtail a splinter taken from the central vertebra of the five-year-old bull Leñizgo. His killing of this animal had won him its ears, tail, four hooves, head, and—as a final and insuperable trophy—its backbone. It was during the faena with Leñizgo that El Porrón, disdaining the adjurations of manager and public to take no chances with that wily and cruel beast, first executed his *paso de las estrellas*, in which the bull passes directly over the fighter's prone body.

During the sittings I observed, M. Namque painted most of the time in a normal manner. Occasionally, however, he would disappear for a moment behind a broad curtain of gray velvet from which, through an elastic slit worked halfway between its center and right edge, a lense-tipped tube stuck out. A faint humming from behind the curtain accompanied these brief withdrawals.

For reasons of temperament, M. Namque and I were drawn to each other from our first meeting. We dined together several times and rapidly came to treat each other as friends. My conversations with him provided a happy outlet for the anxiety that had soured the recent months of my life; and it was no doubt to divert me from my preoccupations that Félix one day delighted me by proposing to reveal his secret and controversial techniques. That evening, after El Porrón had left, he took me behind the velvet curtain.

Half of the concealed space, perhaps thirty square

feet in all, contained a large machine that suggested a specialist's device for sounding some invisible organ. Its case of gray enameled metal was, on the side facing us (opposite the one by the curtain) fitted with a pane of clear glass that exposed the mechanism within. Above the pane, two bands of eleven silver switches were fitted to the lateral rim of the case. Twin viewers, somewhat penny-arcadian, rose from the upper surface of the machine, one at the center, the other towards the right-hand edge, while at an equivalent distance to the left a tubular knee, similarly attached, extended its horizontal shaft through the curtain slit. (It was the other end of this tube, fitted with a lense, that I had observed in the studio.) The machine had no other external features except, at each end, for a thick cord of rubber-covered wire that crossed the floor to a base-plug.

Behind the pane of glass lay an apparently simple apparatus. Its chief component was an arrangement of metal tubing, of a thickness of several inches, that had the shape of a trident. The left-hand prong of tube was attached to the lense-tipped knee; the other two were attached to the viewers. The outermost prongs and the base of the trident comprised one unbroken piece of tubing, while the central prong, a separate length, was hermetically joined to the first.

The two outer shafts of tubing were each fitted with eleven metallic cups that occupied the spaces between the tube-system and the ends of the case. The cups were all wired, every wire being connected first to one of the twenty-two switches of the two panels and ultimately to the external cords.

Félix explained how the machine functioned. The

image received by the lense in the studio was transmitted throughout the trident-shaped tubes by a series of mirrors fixed within them. The transmitted image underwent two alterations. As it passed down the left-hand shaft, appropriate bulbs in the metal cups, which opened on the shaft's interior, subjected the image to a battery of adverse colored lights that acted as an optical sieve, straining all natural color out. The image at this stage was observable in the viewer surmounting the central shaft of tubing; the primary function of this viewer was to determine by observation exactly which lights (controlled by the leftmost panel of switches) were needed to reduce the colored image to grayness.

The straining lamps were termed by Félix *rejectors.*

Thus neutralized, the image entered the right-hand shaft of tube. Again it was subjected to a series of colored lights, but, in distinction to the first set, these infused new colors into the image. The recolored image appeared in the viewer on the right, while the switches below it controlled the second group of lights.

The color-infusing lamps were called *projectors.*

The machine itself, of Félix's own invention, had been baptized *chromaturge.* Félix was understandably pleased with it; its final images were the inexhaustible source of his notorious color-schemes.

In order to produce a freshly colored image, the chromaturge required one decision of its operator—the choice of projectors. At the very start Félix had had to decide before the machine was built what his gamut of colored lights was to be. He had preferred to make this selection once and for all; so rather than use colored bulbs which could, when replaced, tempt him to modify his palette, he had had immovable colored panes, with white bulbs behind them, fixed along the shaft's inner surface. The panes represented a familiar pattern. The numbered switches controlled the following hues:

1. White (= light)
2. Black (= dark)
3. Yellow
4. Red
5. Pink
6. Chocolate
7. Gold
8. Fire-red
9. Violet
10. Blue
11. Purple

The next question was how to pick from this sequence of colors the ones to be used in a particular instance. Félix was again averse to letting chance or taste decide. He considered many systematic approaches, based on the size, shape, age, sex and chemistry of the subject to be painted. In the end he discarded them all as unsatisfactory. The painting, he decided, had its own independent existence; therefore the painting, not the subject, would determine the colors. Félix considered three facts to be of fundamental relevance to the painting's existence: the date and hour of the painting's "birth," the phase of the moon at the time of the painting's "conception," and its price. He used the figures representing these facts as his color-scheme.

The only option he permitted himself was the number of colors employed. The exploitation of all three facts usually brought all eleven colors into play, albeit in descending order of importance, while the use of one or two elements, or even a part of the first one (the date without the hour) allowed of a simpler color-scheme.

Félix illustrated his procedure with the case of El Porrón.

The bullfighter's first sitting had been on the 10 brumaire An CLXIV. (Félix used the revolutionary calendar in honor of his ancestor.) This date, figured as 10/2/164, yielded the colors 10 (blue), 2 (black), 1 (white), 4 (red), and 8 (chocolate). These then were the dominant tones of the portrait. The torero's face and hands were a gorgeous blue, while his costume was a glittering chocolate that, thanks to the chiaroscuro shading introduced by tones 1 and 2, stood strikingly free of a dull red background.

The sitting had begun at 10:07 in the morning. This number involved only the seventh switch, the tenth being already in use. Gold had glowingly touched El Porrón's nails, eyes and teeth—the latter providing that "anchor in the real" that critics hailed in all of Félix's otherwise baffling works.

The "conception" of the portrait—a phonecall offering the commission—had occurred a few weeks prior to the first sitting, under the third phase of the moon; the third switch had given the bullfighter flaxen hair and lemony stockings.

Finally, the price agreed on—1,198,500 francs—had introduced certain finishing details: purple buttons, violet spangles, the fire-red bone splinter, and three pink rings.

Félix had mentioned the price sulkily—it was about half what he usually asked. Questioned on this point, he bitterly remarked that it was not the first time he had made such a sacrifice for the sake of art. Further questioning extracted the confession that he had created near scandals by insisting on prices that were "inevitably high"; that he had postponed the start of one portrait for weeks, almost losing an important client thereby, until a certain "appropriate day"; and that once he had left a hospital bed with pneumonia and a fever of 104° to begin a still life of imperishable objects "before it was too late."

These admitted subterfuges confirmed my growing suspicion that Félix used his system to achieve and justify what he felt like doing. The one uncontrollable number, and then only in such cases as El Porrón's, was that of the work's "conception." But when I suggested that he might have waited to start his portrait until the convenient moment of 10:07 because he wanted to give the torero golden eyes, he was indignant. I listened to his harangue on the impersonality and rigor of his system, then changed the subject.

Yet I was not convinced, and my belief that Félix's system was only a means of supplying him with material for the exercise of his talent was unexpectedly confirmed when he let me look through the two viewers of his machine: the images of his studio that I beheld were exactly alike, and what is more, they were unaltered replicas of what appeared, through the spread curtain, to my naked eye.

As for Roland de la Platière, Félix could not himself

help me. But he told me of a document that, as he remembered, might well touch on the matter. It was a letter that Roland had written to a French lady shortly before his death; her heirs, long afterwards, had returned it to Roland's family. Félix had last heard of it when it was taken to the United States by his cousin, Roland's only other living descendant. Félix gave me his name and address, and a letter of introduction.

I was pleased with this development, for I had good reason already to return to America. My appearance in probate court with such evidence as I had would certainly strengthen my claim to Mr. Wayl's fortune; and in addition I wished once more to see my wife, who had recently begun proceedings against me for divorce. So, in early December, after a farewell celebration at the Café Chien, Félix drove me to Le Havre to board my ship home.

AN EX-BOOK

My other affairs settled, I left New York for Florida where, at Hialeah, I easily found Félix's cousin, Bunuel Namque-Schlendrian. This tiny, much traveled man, fifteen years older than Félix, was as kind to me as his younger relative. After reading through my letter of introduction, he embraced me as if I were a long-lost friend.

At Namque-Schlendrian's insistence, I spent several days as his guest. I believe his hospitality was engendered by the extraordinary turn his fortunes had just taken; for if his pretext for having me stay was a de-sire for news of Félix, whom he had not seen in twenty-five years, his true motive was certainly a natural eagerness to share new happiness with a new acquaintance. It was not long before I became as intimate with him as I had with his cousin; and so I learned the story of Bun's life, which had culminated in success on the very eve of my arrival.

As his name indicated, Namque-Schlendrian was descended through his mother from General Schlendrian, the officer who in the late stages of the Franco-Prussian War had organized an exceptionally effective corps from the troops recruited during his service in Algeria. Among all the "fog of war" no unit harassed the invaders so brilliantly; the reason for their effectiveness, expert training and tactical flair aside, lay in the devotion the Arab troops bore their chief. When Schlendrian's Fellahs were disbanded after the armistice, they further proved this devotion by a communal gift to the general of twenty million Red Sea cowries. (These shells, whose scientific name is *Cypraea turdus*, were once highly valued by many North African tribes.)

The Schlendrian family was then rich. Foolish speculation, bad luck and the dissipations of several members reduced the estate, by the time Namque-Schlendrian was born, to a poor fraction of its former size. His parents died while he was in school, leaving him on his own at the age of seventeen with only a modest inheritance to his advantage. (His only relative was Félix, poor himself.) This inheritance amounted to a small country place in the Beauce; an apartment in Paris; a few books; furniture; and the twenty million cowries.

Restless, solitary and young, Namque-Schlendrian considered what he might make of his life with necessary coolness and rare open-mindedness. Certain ethnoconchological studies persuaded him that he could do better than work respectably at a dull and illpaid office job. Selling his country house and its furnishings for ready cash, he set out with fifty cases of cowries on his long travels.

A steamer took him to Melbourne, whence he proceeded north to Brisbane, there hiring a small boat that brought him around the northeastern Australian coast to Arnhem Land. With a guide and several porters, he traveled inland until, after two weeks, he came to his first goal, the encampment of the Aulayulia tribe. These aborigines used shell money for their trading; their common currency was the cowrie—not the *Cypraea turdus*, but the Indian cowrie, *Cypraea caput serpentis*. They were nevertheless familiar with the *Cypraea turdus*. It seems that at some moment in their past they had traded with a people who bartered the rarer Red Sea shell and had come into possession of a small quantity of it. This store had through loss and theft been so diminished through the countless years that the foreign cowries, held precious from the moment of their acquisition, had assumed a practically sacred value. Namque-Schlendrian hoped to profit from this.

He negotiated for three months with the Aulayulia chieftains. The notion that there could exist so many "rare" shells at first appalled them into a hesitant confusion; but Namque-Schlendrian's patience allowed their reverence for the cowries to reassert its sway, and he finally exchanged his shells for two hundred and fifty million Indian cowries.

Namque-Schlendrian returned to Melbourne to embark with his six hundred and twenty-five cases for Zanzibar. Thence he trekked to the country north of Unyamwezi where he traded his Indian cowries for six hundred and fifty million money cowries (*Cypraea moneta*). He and his one thousand six hundred and twenty-five cases then journeyed by sea around the Cape of Good Hope and up the West African coast, disembarking at Buea in the Cameroons. Traveling inland once more, in a northeasterly direction, he shortly reached the banks of the river Yo. With the Negroes of the region he made a final exchange (transport costs rendered further exploitation of shell values unprofitable). The value assigned to the money cowrie in Western Africa was five times that of the East Coast: The Yo natives estimated Bun's shells as worth twenty-eight pounds thirteen ounces of gold, which they paid; Namque-Schlendrian ended his first wanderings, just as his supply of cash ran out, with the rewarding sum of fourteen thousand dollars.

This money, while worth treble its present value, was certainly no fortune; but it provided Namque-Schlendrian with what he needed most—a small capital to invest when an exceptional opportunity appeared. Now Namque-Schlendrian had already noted such an opportunity, and he decided to take advantage of it immediately.

Namque-Schlendrian admitted that in this matter his good sense had, after a while, given way to an almost monomaniac obstinacy. He could have abandoned his scheme once he recognized the obstacles to realizing it. Instead, he endured for its sake ill health, poverty and humiliation.

During his sojourn in Australia, Namque-Schlendrian, who was versed in the history of horseracing, had learned that Cartesian Diver and Fink's Folly, both descendants of Pettifog from Lala (although through different lines), had arrived in Sydney to be set to stud. Pettifog had, in his offspring from Lala, transmitted a curious set of minor deformations that had first appeared in his ancestor Gypsum. Namque-Schlendrian had been convinced by a study of the ancestry of these horses that they would become fine runners if properly handled.

A brief genealogy of the animals involved is in order. Spurius, the son of Pettifog from Lala by Breastbone from Armchair by Gladstone from Rippe-van-Winkle by Whig from Nutcracker Suite by Gypsum from White Loss, sired Cartesian Diver from Latest Sin, who, shipped to Australia, there sired Melancthon from Greta Garbo, Spelling Bee from Periphrasis, Black Dick from Penal Servitude, and Ticktock from Asylum. Pettifog also sired from Lala several mares. The most successful of these was Cunning, who threw Brickbat to Fug, who sired the Derby winner Krach from Liliom, and Zazz to Horse, who threw in turn the handicap champion Hangover to Lordy Me. Another mare was named Fink's Folly; she was sent to Australia with Cartesian Diver, and there threw Flibbetigibbet, Pounce, and Excitation to Jinglebells, all of which raced poorly. Among the mares she foaled were Crass Delight, June Filly, Poontang, Gattamalatta, and, lastly, Grave Lady. The latter's sire, Lugstone, who had been set to Maryjohn, was by Celtic

Doom from Alba Longa by Fissure from Would-to-God by Bloody Bastard from Pity Palace. In Australia, before being bought by Namque-Schlendrian she threw Schwarzwald to Plexus; under Bun's ownership she threw six colts to Ticktock—Triple X, Frosty Mikado, Buckwheat Blues, Watchstopper's Gusset, Bulldog Lemny, and Winged Cribbage; and two fillies—Wilder Membership and Commie Coup.

Originally Namque-Schlendrian planned to buy Cartesian Diver and Fink's Folly. In order to learn the trade, he returned to Australia and went to work at the farm where the two horses were at stud, first as hotwalker, later as groom and exercise boy. A series of disasters wrecked his plans. At the end of his second year, he was thrown by a horse, fracturing his skull in the fall. Namque-Schlendrian spent eight months in a coma and two years recovering. Resuming his duties, he performed them satisfactorily for another year and was ready to turn owner when, overcome by one of the spells of giddiness that followed his accident, he so mismanaged his mount that the horse broke a leg under him and had to be shot. Since this animal was a prize three-year-old, Namque-Schlendrian was obliged to compensate its owner (a niggardly parvenu with a loud disbelief in insurance) with a large sum; and when he tried to make up his loss with a few heavy bets at the track, bad luck reduced what was left of his stake to less than three thousand dollars. Still undismayed, he went on at his job hoping, since he earned a good wage, to save enough for his purpose. His savings had by 1940 grown to the equivalent of eleven thousand dollars. In the summer of that year they were seized with the bank accounts of all French residents upon the formation of the Pétain government. At first interned, Namque-Schlendrian later served honorably in the war as a liaison officer for the Far Eastern Gaullist platoon. His services failed to recover his money, or at least not its true value. It was transferred to France at the prewar rate of exchange, under an agreement between the Free French and Australian governments, and its buying power had fallen, by the time Namque-Schlendrian could use it, to about fifteen hundred dollars. Even this could not be taken out of France.

The following three years were the saddest of Namque-Schlendrian's life. He went back to work at the stable, but despondently, not knowing what else to do. No longer an inspiration, his obsession had become a dead weight he dragged hopelessly about. Cartesian Diver and Fink's Folly were now both dead. In their place his choice had fallen on their foals Ticktock and Grave Lady. When these horses were sold and sent to the United States, Namque-Schlendrian managed to accompany them as groom. In less than a year he had lost this job because of his growing carelessness, the result of recurring depressions. He then joined a small organization of bookmakers in which, thanks to his native acumen, he was able to make a modest living until his luck turned.

His good fortune came from an unexpected quarter. In the fall of 1950, Félix wrote him a letter telling him of the current demand for apartments in Paris and advising him to let his, long vacant. Authorized to act on his cousin's behalf, Félix made a few minimal repairs and soon had a tenant. The apartment was attractively situated: a comfortable soundproofed studio in the tower of the church of St. Germain-des-Prés. Namque-Schlendrian began receiving monthly cheques of five hundred, a thousand, and, finally, two thousand dollars. In less than three years he was the owner of a well-staffed stud farm in Fayette County, Kentucky, where Grave Lady had already thrown Ticktock his first colt, Triple X.

Only the day before I arrived in Hialeah Triple X had made and won his initial start, running three furlongs in 0:32⅖, finishing eleven lengths in front of the second horse, and confirming his owner's twenty-five-year-old hunch.

Gypsum and certain of his offspring, notably the descendants of Pettifog and Lala, were known for certain external peculiarities—slightly curby hocks, lop ears and high withers. Namque-Schlendrian believed, at first after a long study of their past performances, later from observation, that these visible characteristics were accompanied by a certain organic deformation. As owner of Ticktock and Grave Lady he found his hypothesis exact. In both these horses and, subsequently, in their foals, the splanchnic nerve, which controls the adrenal gland, passed in abnormal fashion through the coil of the large intestine on its way from medulla to kidney. Namque-Schlendrian reasoned that the nerve was stimulated, and the production of adrenalin increased, when the horse's intestines were exceptionally swollen—that is, when the horse was constipated; and he believed this fact might provide the realization of the racing bug's dream—the undetectable fix.

A less talented man might have failed to use such knowledge properly. With patience, imagination and pluck, Namque-Schlendrian succeeded in the formidable task of training a horse to constipate himself voluntarily at set times. At his farm he determined the delicate intervals (varying with every horse) between feeding, the onset of constipation and the running of the race. He had seen his methods justified in his private time trials: when properly costive, Triple X, his very soul soaked in adrenalin, surpassed his best "free" performances. The colt's first race had of course been the supreme test, and Triple X's victory a supreme consolation for Namque-Schlendrian's years of ignominy. The suspicions of the judges, amazed at the colt's performance, were allayed by the official analyses, which showed that no drug had been administered nor illegal physical stimulus applied. The bookmakers who had been his partners were also surprised—Namque-Schlendrian collected from them the fruits of two thousand dollars invested at twenty-two to one. (Even the odds had been favored by his machinations: in the paddock, the beginnings of the adrenalin attack had put Triple X in such a sweat that he scared away many of his potential backers.)

Such was Namque-Schlendrian's history as he told it to me. He gave me an additional mark of confidence after he had finished his tale by revealing yet another trade secret. This was a stopwatch that he had had made to fit under the instep of his foot; it was operated by moving the great toe. The hidden contraption gave Namque-Schlendrian easy access to the jealously guarded time trials of his competitors. The results of these trials were precious information, and no responsible owner or trainer invited anyone to them out of politeness or friendship. Namque-Schlendrian's charm had won him a privileged place in the society of owners. By making a point of never carrying or using a stopwatch, or even an ordinary watch, he persuaded his colleagues that there was no danger in his witnessing their tryouts, rather an opportunity to show off their horses to an appreciative connoisseur.

Namque-Schlendrian had given Jean-Marie Roland's letter to the Canossa Washington Library of Fitchwinder University in Swetham, Massachussetts. Since only specialists were allowed to consult the manuscript collection of which the letter was now a part, Namque-Schlendrian wrote on my behalf to the library director, thus advancing my investigations greatly.

During my last afternoon in Hialeah, I payed a farewell call on Namque-Schlendrian in his office suite at the track.

He showed me his collections of souvenirs and curiosities, among them a medieval muleteer's packsaddle that had been given to him by none other than Mr. Wayl. I recognized on it a familiar design. Worked long ago into the cracked leather, it was still legible: a naked woman stood near the mouth of a stream by a mound of cowrie shells. The scene was identical with the one engraved on the point of my adze, except that on the saddle the woman was depicted from behind. Mr. Wayl had led me to believe that this scene was merely decorative; yet here it was underscored with the inscription, *Cypriae Sedes Gloria Regis*, while the other side of the saddle bore the arms of the "false Johnstones," with an added mark—a band that crossed the shield from the upper right corner to the center and then descended to its point.

After quitting Bun (he knew nothing at all about the saddle: Mr. Wayl had given it to him because of his knowledge of cowries) I proceeded to Boston and to nearby Swetham, where I spent a day in the study of Roland's letter. Mr. Meniscus, the library director, has forbidden me to reproduce its text, but he has most kindly authorized the translation that follows.

ROLAND TO MADAME MIOT (I)

chez Mlle Malortie,
dans la rue de l'Ours,
Rouen.

Le 9 Brumaire, An II.

Madam,

I write in a state of dejection such as I have not known in many years. So much time has passed since your letter came—and such time! It has exhausted my life, and me; I have passed through multiples of anguish; I have yearned for peace, then resignation, and afterwards hopelessness, but it seems there is no passivity in despair—the insomniac quest for death is an ascent into pain. I live now—well, I am simply alive. I try to order what is still mine, although there is no distraction in it; and so I shall answer your queries. I am thankful that my matter will give me words to send you; my brain is in truth quite blank otherwise, except for what is unspeakable.

I have indeed "visited Egypt," like my old namesake, perhaps learning there more than even he; and I did not have to cross water to reach it. I think you know the manner of my acquaintance with those people, and the depth of my attachment. As for the history, I can offer fragments only—the records are few, many have been lost or destroyed. There have, however, been certain letters, whose details—with due prudence—can be enriched with familiar lore; and the facts admitted into official texts—*quegli scritti lugubri che fanno tornare eternamente i morti!*—must in turn be introduced, and then we have—not a history, but bright glimpses of a history: like a winter moon in the chance openings of snow-clouds.

In the year 1410 a clan of Wallachian Gypsies came to Scotland from the Continent. They preceded the mass of their race by nearly a century; for among their own people they were renegades. Small, dark, quick-footed, they resembled their fellow Gypsies in physique, and like them, they raised horses and cattle. It was their religion that marked them. They had preserved the practice of an old cult dedicated to Sylvius of Alba Longa, and they worshiped him as a divine hero, and as their king. In their version of the legend,

Sylvius was no son of Aeneas but a bastard offspring of Lavinia, fathered by a god whose name could never be mentioned or written down. There is nothing I can tell you of the origins and growth of the sect in antiquity, or of its history during the first thirteen centuries of Christianity: the tale must be discovered by a more enlightened age that will recognize wisdom in the diligence of the learned. My knowledge begins with the establishment of the sect in Scotland, and the first celebrations there of its mysteries, in a shrine that lay not far from the town of Allova (*sic*), in the year 1411.

The new shrine received Sylvius's name—a name belonging not only to the legendary hero, but given as a title to the successive chiefs of the Gypsies, whom they called kings. They believed that Sylvius was immortal in the bodies of these kings, and that he sanctified them by his presence. In 1411 Alexander Stewart, a recent convert to the sect, and its protector, bore the name. Like every king he was born in bastardy of noble stock; and he had been *chosen.*

For Sylvius, god or man, was not the supreme ruler: that authority belonged to the "Queen" whose vicegerent he was. She is an obscure power. Unlike the king's, her office was not perpetually renewed—she was supposedly a divine being who from time to time, when the need arose, appeared among her worshipers as a mere woman. I cannot say how often she manifested herself, or how she was recognized. Only one of her peculiarities is known: she was nearly always gifted with some Negro blood.

All the shrines of the sect were established for the performance of her rites. Concerning one of these, the

Flaying of the King, I know more than a little. It was performed in the glen near Allova, on Hallowe'en and All Hallows' Day, a year after the Gypsies' arrival.

The gathering of the sect took place during the morning of the first day. Most of those that came were Gypsies, but there were many Scots and English lately converted, and an even greater number of earlier converts from the countries of Europe. The first business was the publication and discussion of the year's accounts. During the afternoon there were numerous private ceremonies of marriage, burial and initiation.

The marriage ceremony culminated in the eating by the bride and the groom of a small cake made out of malt, rye and lard together with bits of hair clipped from the sacred parts of their bodies—loins, armpit, and head.

The blessing of the dead consisted in clothing the corpses (preserved through the year for this occasion) with fresh ash leaves, then sprinkling them with a powder of dried bdellium gum.

Children brought for initiation were similarly sprinkled. I do not know the practice relating to adult initiates.

Towards evening, the king, dressed in mean clothes, approached the sacred ashtree. He was there stripped by seven seven-year-old boys, and bitten by seven seven-year-old dogs. He stood before the Queen, who was accompanied by a young woman carrying a bowl of liquid bdellium gum, and by a young man who in one hand held a gisarme, which they called an adze (*une hallebarde que l'on appelait herminette*), in the other a wooden effigy of the king. The effigy, about three feet high, had been grotesquely carved from a piece of white poplar and afterwards smoked black; a metal point was attached to its base. The adze was made of gold, fitted with an iron edge.

The young man, planting the effigy in the ground, began lopping off its projecting members one by one with the adze. As each part fell, the Queen smeared the same part of the king with gum, until the effigy had been reduced to a straight white bolt and the king had been anointed all over his body. A second young man approached, carrying a crossbow. He drew the wooden shaft from the earth, set it in his bow, and shot it into the trunk of the ashtree. As soon as a leaf fell from the tree, all withdrew but the king, who was left alone, naked and erect under the tree, its leaves falling on him through the night. His followers did not sleep but wandered at a distance through the woods surrounding the glen. Those newly married on beds of leaves consummated or confirmed their marriage. The blessed corpses were deposed in holy streams and caves.

(What did the Queen do during that night? According to some, she returned to the king to sleep with him. Others say she murdered and replaced him, out of sight of all.)

The ashtree shed all its leaves in that one night, many of them falling on the king and adhering to his gummy limbs. In the morning the entire sect, gathered anew, finds the tree bare and their king glued with ashleaves. The Queen comes to him and leads him to a nearby spring, where she washes him and herself (she is naked) a first time. Once more she rubs the king with gum, mixed with seven hundred appleseeds. Then she daubs herself completely with mud from the ground near the spring, to which the young woman again attending her adds petals of bloody-fingers (*doigts de la Vierge*). The king and Queen return to the ashtree's foot, where their followers await them in neat ranks. The young woman now opens many boxes containing tiny gray butterflies, gathered during the summer months and carefully saved; while the young man, the destroyer of the king's effigy, looses a large flock of bullfinches from a cage in the ashtree's lower branches. The butterflies alight by the hundred on the muddy Queen, covering her in so close a robe she seems a statue of pale gray fur. The bullfinches attack the king to peck off his coat of seeds. Their hard bills pierce him in many places, and the king bleeds: all the believers come forward in an orderly file to kiss his blood. They cannot touch the Queen, kissing instead the ground before her. (But since her eyes are covered, she does not see this homage.) After a while the butterflies, unfit for November air, fall off dying. The Queen leads the bloody king back to the spring, washes him, and clothes him in his royal suit of leather leaves. She has first cleansed herself, and put on a black goat surplice lined entirely with white catskins. On the lining's border a motto has been sewn with thread wound out of rhubarb fibers. The motto† reads: *Aeneas Nothus Rex: Rex Nothus Sylvius*. Beneath her surplice the Queen is naked, save for her garter of puffballs, and goes barefoot. The worshipers this morning all wear hats, and many sport on their belts sprigs of bubon, St. John's wort and verbena.

The Queen at last crowned the king, or, rather, presented him with his crown, which was a wreath of clematis. The couple then received from each of their followers a vow of fidelity and a small offering in money or kind.

The royal pair led the way to a cleared space. Around it the newfallen ashleaves were heaped in a ring and lighted. Damp and still full of sap, their fire filled the air with tart thick smoke. The king started to sing through his nose, producing a roaring wooden voice; he accompanied himself by rattling a bell of horn with his right hand, and beating with his left a human bone on a horse's skull. This was the sign to begin the Parodies, of which, alas, I can only describe two, the first and last of the many performed.

The opening parody was of a foxhunt. A fox was placed in the center of the clearing, and a pack of hounds set after him. The dogs made themselves foolish, for the fox, made of loosely woven ivy, was invisible to them, and they passed heedlessly through or over it following the trace of a true foxskin that had been dragged across the ground in the pattern of an equilateral triangle, the ivy replica lying at one of its corners.

The closing parody was a joust. Riding blinded sheep, crippled dwarfs met each other in the lists with weapons that, though miniature, were real enough. Perhaps the smoke of the leaves, nearly blinding by then, veiled the bloodiness of the spectacle.[4]

A banquet followed the Parodies. I retain only one of its details.

A shoat prepared for the royal table was filleted with rhubarb thread in such a way that a red letter B appeared on its chest. After the king had tasted the meat of the animal, he stood up and demanded the attention of the company. Then putting a golden boar's head over his own, he opened his suit of leaves to lay bare his chest: the skin between the nipples, unmarked at first, soon showed the trace of a pink B, and the letter affirmed itself until it was a brilliant red.

The banquet over, there was dancing. The king and his nine "abbreviators" opened with a prescribed ritual dance, whose nature I am ignorant of. It appears to have been performed to the accompaniment of a kind of mangle (*avec de la musique issue d'une calandreuse*). Afterwards there was general dancing, to the music of flutes, jew's-harps, harps and oaklog drums.

ROLAND TO MADAME MIOT (II)

In 1456 political circumstances led to the destruction of Sylvius's shrine. A large gang of "orthodox" Gypsies were imported from the Low Countries to do the work; they did it thoroughly. They massacred many of the sect, Gypsy or not. The glen was ravaged, its spring polluted, its sacred tree cut to bits, its royal stone smashed, even its thriving vines uprooted.

It is said that the Queen led the glen's defense, at first by force of arms, later, when the woods had been fired, with pleas for the sparing of her people.[5] She herself was not slain, but made prisoner in the king's name and sent to Rome for trial before high dignitaries of the church. Summarily condemned as a witch, she succeeded in her appeal to the extent of being allowed to present her case to the pope, Pius II.

The pope received her without her judges or her guards, alone except for an actuary who transcribed their interview. Officially destroyed, the transcription was smuggled out and sold to one of the Queen's loyal followers. Here is the version I once saw, or as much of it as I can reconstruct from notes set down at the time.

The Queen. If I forsook the glory of public martyrdom, among the tatters of my people, forsook burning with them, and not leaving them; if I left them, and the other Sylvius and all my children, who will burn alone, or endure the rotting cold of their hills; if I submitted to a king not my king, not fit to be my subject, and submitted to the secular petty fury of moles: it is not because I do not want to burn, but because I want to burn royally. And you shall do the burning—you are fit for that.

The Pope. I granted your request firstly because you are known to me, as I to you; secondly because I am curious (and yet too delicate: that combination has put hopes of happiness beyond me); thirdly because I have a favor to ask of you. It is a trivial favor. You see, a few weeks ago an inexplicable wound opened in my left thigh. It has refused to leave me, and I suffer from it no little.

The Queen. I have come to say what I have to say. I have been speaking for months and those about me hear a devil's voice. They hear it even when I am silent —they cannot understand their terror! You can understand, yet you must listen, for the end must be true to the beginning, and what was born in water must die in fire.

The Pope. Whatever you came for, you are here for my reasons, and chiefly for my wounded thigh. It is strange that it was only a few days ago that I imagined a connection between my wound and your captivity, even though I had just learned you were to be sent here when the ill declared itself. The other day I mentioned the matter lightly to my nephew and he grew very pale. Delegations of well-wishers have appeared at punctual intervals since to advise me, with the most respectful discretion, that I should deal leniently with you. Of course I laughed at all of them. And then I thought, how worried they will be for themselves! They will soon start hunting down poor Gypsies whose looks have happened to cross theirs, there will be murders open and obscure, and sleepless nights, and bad dreams by day, and much time lost. I am sickened by such affairs. Are you my enemy? If you are, you are so less than others: there are remoter lands where error is mightier. So I decided to have you come to me, that you might try to cure me. (The Queen laughed.) Perhaps I should elaborate: you may *try*. It is your certain failure that interests me. Afterwards, the wound will eventually heal of itself. This is a slow answer to your presumptions, but it will wither them wholly.

The Queen. You came out of my belly, you sucked my breasts: noble boy, consider who I am! I have no presumptions but those of my true worship. My soul has been wrapped in honey. I play with curious shells, branches and trusting animals, and with blood and the smells of sperm and the dead. I have no need to work miracles: they happen about me. Your thigh! And your dead mythologies! Does Actaeon or St. Sebastian hallow the dim unease of your pain? Is learning only for fools? When next you pass an anthill, approach it and study its perfection, and think of your failing powers: and think of Alva when they carry you past its leaves . . .

The Pope. Alba no longer. You will hang and not burn;[6] yours is a common offense.

He turned the Queen back to her judges, who submitted her to the Question, as was usual, before ordering her execution. Charged with various acts of malevolent witchcraft, she of course denied them all. The account of her last hours is found in the official transcript of the trial:

The person under examination was first tied with rope; then she was fitted with Spanish boots and stretched out on the ladder; no answers were forthcoming to the questions asked, and her eyes were constantly open. She was dropped from the ladder and raised again. After that she was poured a draught. Then the Spanish boots were tightened. All of the hair of her body was shaved; fire was passed under her nose and behind her ears; afterwards she was again strappadoed, hanging in the air for a whole hour. During this time she remained silent. Later, when she spoke, an appeal to the Devil, who was addressed as Triton, was all she uttered. Her voice was cool, unstrained, and her face colored. She was sprinkled, rubbed and smoked with lighted sulfur; once more she was strappadoed, and she cried out.

The person under examination was extended on the ladder and given a draught. She was burned anew with sulfur. Again she was raised, and another draught, which was swallowed with difficulty, after which she sank down as if she were about to go to sleep. She was again burned with sulfur, under her chin, under her arms, in her secret parts. Again strappadoed. *Triton, have pity on me!* were her only words. After that she was calm for a rather long time, and, although she was called to, there was no answer, gasping as she was, her face still flushed, without tears, however, but only drops of sweat on her forehead.

The person under examination was newly stretched. Then the Spanish boots were screwed tight; and again a draught, which was not swallowed, no matter what means were employed. After which she remained calm, without complaint of any pain.

The person under examination had just been strappadoed once more and rubbed with sulfur, when a gray butterfly began fluttering about her. Seeing it, the person under examination twisted her head towards it so hard that the torturer, with his helpers, could hardly turn it back. The butterfly then flew towards the window, which was half open, and after resting on the sill a while, disappeared outside. At the moment of the butterfly's appearance, the face of the person under examination had become horribly pale, her mouth screwed up, her lips blue; but as soon as the insect disappeared she was completely calm. She was taken off the ladder and lain on some straw. They brought vinegar for her to breathe, but she was dead. The clock had just struck six.

The undersigned, notary public, certifies, &c.

Tota Philosophia, inquit Plato, nihil est aliud, quam quædam commentatio mortis, neque aberrat mea quidem sententia. Cur enim præcepta bene vivendi discimus, nisi ut bene mori sciamus. Comœdia quidem est nostra vita, cuius ultimus actus &c.—so wrote that pope in a later sententious moment. Those who are elevated in this world exude the sublime cruelty of the insane.

Yet the pope relented at last. At the end of the trial minutes the verdict reads (although the Queen was already dead): *Convicta et combusta.*

ROLAND TO MADAME MIOT (III)

Yesterday, to my surprise, I received a long letter about the glen of Allova and its former role as a shrine. The writer was some American crank who had gotten hold of a few facts (even those he garbled). I plan to send him a curt note that should thoroughly deflate him.

Perhaps I am wrong in doing this—there are few enough who show even a misguided interest in poor Sylvius and his Queen. Since that ancient raid on the glen the sect's history has been a sad one: fits of enthusiasm fading into long wastes of abandonment. In our century the apathy of the believers has been such that the Barilone of Massa may fall into ruin.

One of my dearest friends, Jehan de Sfè, among the last members of the sect, went quite mad as a result of its disintegration. Since he had been associated with us politically, he prudently left Paris for Valence last winter; and I payed him a brief visit there. Presenting myself at his villa, I waited for him in the library: after a few minutes Sfè came in, walking backwards, and cried, *Roi vous veut de risée le plaît qu'en l'or rèche homme!* Not making head or tail of this I asked him to repeat what he had said several times and finally to write it down. He did all I asked patiently and courteously. On the slip of paper he handed me I read: *!riov suov ed risialp leuq dnaloR rehc noM.* He had written this reverse sentence as rapidly as I might have written it normally. After I had had him read it aloud —he uttered the same sounds as he had at first done— I understood that he both spoke and wrote backwards, and that in doing so he carefully respected the distinction between the written and the spoken word, even though it was here made singularly arduous: writing, he reversed the letters of his sentences; speaking, he reversed their sounds. Once the necessary civilities were dispensed with, I asked him, fascinated, to recite me several classical tirades. It was with a truly manic grandeur that he pronounced Phèdre's

Et chatte à oir passa ré y tend toutes une Eve est-ce!

Then, knowing Sfè to be a talented musician, I asked him to perform for me. At the harpsichord a similar prodigy occurred: accompanying himself, he sang Rousseau's setting of *Se tu m'ami* from end to beginning with an ease that flabbergasted me. But soon pity and sadness at knowing an old friend lost (for conversation with him was so laborious that it would have been impossible in serious matters) overcame my somewhat unwholesome curiosity; and I took my leave. Sfè's sister wrote me a few months ago that his peculiarity had lasted until the day he had his cataracts couched. The operation not only failed: after a few hours of lucidity, during which he incessantly proclaimed his fidelity to the Queen, it took his life.

On my arrival here, I had charged myself with one final duty, that of ensuring the perpetuation of the Queen's monument. Last week I traveled with it by land as far as Houlgate, there hiring a small fishingboat, which I took out myself, desiring to conceal the nature and destination of my cargo. After rowing for several hours, I happened to pass close to another boat; the fisherman in it, pointing seawards, shouted that if I continued, my goal would be in sight within half an hour. Surprised, I thanked him and rowed on. I spied a small island, whose very existence had been unknown to me (I have since been unable to discover it on any map). The place was rocky, completely uninhabited, and sparsely planted. Several hundred yards from the center of its southern shore I sank the memorial of the Queen in the sea; it now rests in about twenty feet of water.

Since then, except for this letter, I have abandoned all work. It is practically impossible for me to write; but I had expected at least to assemble my new notes on Dictys of Crete and on "myself"—it seems, by the way, that my counterpart did indeed write not ζωδιακοῦ but σεληναίου.

I cannot even weep; I only let fall a few occasional burning tears. I have given up hope for Marie Phlipon, and I have nothing to hope from her, either—I am told she now claims to have always considered me a sexless being! I do not mind her thinking so, but must she declare it so loudly that it reaches my ears? My end is at hand; even so I will not be a burden to others; and you shall remain my example. Those of your stamp have a single law, it is written in their hearts, there too is my rule: engrave my pardon there.

Where is another true heart to be found? I have left my own in a wicked magnet. Πάντα ὕδωρ ἐστί.

In what condition do you now see my soul? How do you judge me? Listen: I am in despair.

Madama, vi riverisco con tanto il cuor.

THALES

(Ten days later Roland, learning of his wife's execution, wandered from Rouen several miles into the countryside, and after pinning to his breast a scrawled explanation of his act, killed himself near Bourg-Beaudoin. He was buried on the spot. Aside from the information it contains, his letter is curious for being addressed to Madame Miot; he had attended the burial of her ashes three years before.)

MISS DRYREIN AND THE BARILONE

From Roland's letter I gleaned a wealth of facts concerning my prize adze. I was confident too that I had found the answer to the will's third question, and I hurried to New York to verify my findings with Miss Dryrein, the executrix, before going to court with them.

But if Miss Dryrein was impressed and satisfied by my ability to explain the adze's significance, she destroyed my hope of having the final answer. My hypothesis was that the old man was King Sylvius; that his beard was that of the boar's head he put on at the Sylvian feast; and that the Gypsies who attacked the glen literally or symbolically shaved it, probably by castrating the king.

Miss Dryrein dismissed this theory with a simple No. Without explanation, she showed me a movie Mr. Wayl had taken during one of his trips. Isidore Fod, who had accompanied Mr. Wayl (long before the scandal that ruined his career), spoke a commentary to it:

We are going to see various details of the Barilone, that strange underground palace unearthed this summer near Massa Marittima, west of Siena. The closeup shows how the discovery was made. When large deposits of lignite were found in the region, mining operations were begun in great haste so as to relieve the area's chronic unemployment. Some miners were working a vein of mundic when they came upon these giant ants that we see here, extracting brasses (as they call pyrites crystals) from the surrounding material. When the miners tried to find out where the ants came from, they accidentally opened a hole in the ceiling of the Barilone. Unfortunately two workers fell through the hole. Now we see a parade led by a band with its banner reading *Fanfara di Vicq d'Azyr*—he was one of the miners killed, the one who opened up the hole. Of course the discovery brought quite a lot of tourism to the town, and even temporary prosperity—hence the parade. Here we see Signor Grembo-Maledetti, the president of the mining company, inaugurating the entrance to the Barilone. The name *Barilone*, which means big vat, derives from the shape of the palace, which consists of one enormous barrel-vaulted hall. Its walls are covered with interesting frescoes. Here is a sample of them. In the leftmost of these three paintings we see a clearing ringed with vine-covered trees. A group of vagabonds attacks a gathering of gentlefolk at a sumptuous outdoor banquet. In the right-hand painting we have the same scene after the attackers have left—the ground covered with the bodies of the slain, the trees cut down or burned: no living thing, animal or plant, remains. Unfortunately the middle space has been badly damaged, and one cannot see what happens there.

The reel ended. Turning on the lights, Miss Dryrein looked at me questioningly; but I did not understand. She shook her head resignedly, and her attention to my predicament ebbed augustly.

A few months later I visited Massa myself, to see if there were no visible remnants of that "middle" fresco.

At the Massa chamber of commerce an official gave me a note and told me to proceed to the house of Monroè Fesso, custodian of the Barilone. Signor Fesso lived near the coalmines that now deface the hills behind Massa. As I approached the front door, framed with dried twigs, of his modest marble house, I noticed a curious chirruping noise, to which I paid no attention. Before I was close enough to knock, however, the chirruping faded away: the ensuing quiet was almost startling. Sig. Fesso then appeared around one corner of the house. Noticing my bemused expression, he at once explained to me what had produced the noise and its disappearance. Despite its proximity to the mines, the local electrical company had not laid its cables as far as Sig. Fesso's house. Unable to install a doorbell for the many tourists needing his services, the guardian of the

Barilone had found a novel substitute. The dried twigs framing the door were not twigs at all, but hundreds of tan grasshoppers tied to each other and fastened to the door-frame like a vine. Under normal circumstances the grasshoppers kept up a lively racket, but at the approach of a visitor they would fall silent; and this silence was an effective summons to Sig. Fesso, even when he was on the far side of his house. (Indeed, that was where my arrival had found him. He had been in his vegetable garden, doing his spring digging. Noticing that he wore a strange vest of leather fitted with thin close-set iron spikes, I asked him its function. With some embarrassment he explained that he used it to smooth the worked earth: after digging each patch he would roll over it, his vest then quickly and efficiently filling the office of a rake. Its only drawback, he said, was that it dirtied him—he was in fact smirched from head to foot.)

Sig. Fesso directed the way to the entrance of the Barilone, a Babylonian concrete portal. Its lintel bore an inscription that began *Inaugurato da Silvio Grembo-Maledetti* . . . and gave the date and a brief prose poem. On the cement flag before the door I remarked two parallel X's about ten inches long, which I took to be the mark of Mr. Wayl's presence at the inauguration; for he was known to sport shoes mounted on X-shaped springs.

As he passed through the door Sig. Fesso curtly bowed his head, saying: Amen! A dark corridor in the hillside led to the Barilone proper, a semicylindrical hall a hundred yards long, forty yards wide, and fifteen yards high down its center. Halfway to the far end a metal partition divided the hall into equal parts, but it was perforated with so many intersecting abstract designs it scarcely troubled one's view. On either side of this screen vertical bands of frescoes had been painted, those nearest it identical in width and disposition, those farther from it increasingly disparate and irregular as they approached the ends of the hall. Most of the frescoes had been so mutilated as to be illegible—a general desquamation had marred every surface of the Barilone; but in some cases, where the paint itself had fallen, their drawings, in Cologne earth, were still apparent.

One painting, nearly intact, showed an ecclesiastical figure gloating over a book presented to him by a liveried servant who had opened it at the title-page. The only recognizable words of the title were: *vatter der bapst Pius*. Pope Pius was drawn in curious caricature like a jack of spades.

Of another fresco, only a signature remained, neatly spelled: *Bernardinvs Pintvrichivs Pervsinvs*.

In a third fresco, a bishop who lifted his eyes sanctimoniously heavenwards held out his arms in benediction over a mob engaged in stoning with oyster-shells a proud bloodied woman.

The "middle" fresco of Mr. Wayl's movie was underneath this scene. I examined it with my flashlight. All I found was the outline of certain tendrils near the bottom of the picture, one of which bore the remains of greenish-white coloring; reaching down from above, a hand clutched the tendrils.

I called over Sig. Fesso, who had sat down next to the entrance to read *Tintin en Amérique*, and asked him to identify the subjects of the "middle" fresco and the one over it. Asked who the sanctimonious bishop was, he said:

Che grillo! Amen.

Of the stoned woman: *Che pazzia!* Amen.

Of the plants in the "middle" fresco: *Alba!* Amen.

His first two answers angered me, the third released all the fury of months of hope and labor made vain. Crying out: So it's Alva! Enough of Alva!, I grabbed poor Sig. Fesso by the throat and knocked him on the head with my flashlight. I think I should have killed him if the pain inflicted by the spikes of his gardening vest had not made me let him drop. Leaving him unconscious on the ground, I fled, weeping with shame and disappointment, from the Barilone and from Massa.

Monroè Fesso quickly recovered from my violence —I learned as much from the next day's paper. I was sorry I could not atone for my behavior, especially as reflection had convinced me that his answers were not the impertinences I had taken them to be. What I heard as *Che grillo!* and (forgetting the position of the tonic accent) *Che pazzia!* had surely been *Cirillo* and *Ipazia*, protagonists in just such a scene as that fresco portrayed. Had he perhaps meant something else too by *Alba?*

ALL THINGS ARE WATER

I had fled to Rome: thence I traveled by plane to Paris, and on to Houlgate by train. My hope, my last hope, was that an inspection of Roland's monument to the Queen might lead to the answer I could not find otherwise.

Roland's unmapped island had come out of obscurity—it was none other than Cliff-le-Bone, the vacation resort. An efficient ferry service set me on it the same morning I arrived in Houlgate. It was early in the summer, and there were few tourists; but among those, I was lucky enough to find a group of amateur skin-divers, called the Cogito Swimmers Club, who had picked Cliff-le-Bone for their yearly outing. As their name implied, the Cogito Swimmers were interested in more than the practical aspects of skindiving—they believed that prolonged immersion helped introspection and metaphysical speculations; yet they were delighted to help me look for the monument.

That afternoon, we hired a boat at one of the twelve piers forming the island's pleasant harbor. I let the Swimmers lead the search, for I was inexpert in handling myself underwater and in reconnoitering the submarine landscape.

Following them, I reflected on a telegram forwarded to me earlier in the day at the island's hotel. My lawyers in New York informed me that the letter I had studied at Fitchwinder University was not in Roland's hand and had been declared a forgery; that consequently Mr. Wayl's will had been thrown out as a complete hoax; and that Beatrice and Isidore Fod were to inherit the fortune. I had promptly decided to fight these decisions. Now, gliding through a cold lunar world, I found my confidence waning. The undersea manifested its effect on my brain, as the Cogito Swimmers had described it: memories flooded my head.

Was not Mr. Wayl, whose eccentricity had been demonstrated at his own funeral, capable of forging Roland's letter, and a history's worth of documents as well? What of the poem Professor Bumbè had shown me and its faint odor of anachronism? Who had ever heard of the novel in which I had read of the Johnstones, with its view of life so unlike the warm Auerbach's? Was Abe Johnstone's preposterous letter also a "plant"? Mr. Wayl had the money to bribe town clerks and customs officials and musicologists into helping him. He could have hired without any trouble a "policeman" to keep me out of the Silver Glen. As for the Voe-Doges's painting, were they not his relatives? And since Mr. Wayl knew Namque-Schlendrian (to whom he had given the saddle showing the Queen's birthplace), perhaps he also knew Namque. If I could not believe that Félix and Bun had wittingly tricked me, they might well have been involuntary accomplices. For Mr. Wayl must have foreseen the path my research would inevitably follow, and he could accordingly set along it trap after trap. As to why he should play such an elaborate trick on me, I was at a loss—a modest if dilettantish mulatto hardly seemed prey worthy of such trouble. Yet I felt that I had, at the end of long folly, reached the sad truth, the truth of my delusion. As we hunted over the rough Atlantic floor, I was sure we should find nothing.

Having inspected fields of squat crags, we arrived at a sandy patch, strewn only with shingle and lesser shells, except for one hump of stone rising in the center of that place. An unstony suppleness on the surface of the hump caught my attention, and beckoning to the other swimmers, who were already proceeding, I led the way to it. The seeming rock stood at least ten feet high. As soon as we were next to it, we saw that its stoniness was an illusion created by profuse sea growths that grayly clothed what lay beneath them —a clumsy jumble of hawsers and smaller ropes, piled over the inverted skeleton of a dory. We set to work removing this slimy covering. It was not necessary to move the waterlogged wreck to see what had been hidden underneath.

A thumb-shaped structure,[7] six feet high and four feet thick, rested on the seafloor, a clocklike mechanism forming the greater part of its mass.

The uppermost part of this mechanism was a screen on which were figured the four quarters of the moon. They were, from left to right, a black disc; a like disc with a segment of white (now yellowed) on its right edge; a white disc; and a black disc with a segment of white on its left edge.

Behind a shield of thin metal that hid its juncture with the machinery below, a slender clock-hand of white wood rose across the panel of moons. The hand's base being fixed, its tip necessarily described an arc of about ninety degrees, moving from the left limb of the leftmost disc to the right limb of the rightmost disc. The exact phase of the moon was shown by the point on which the hand rested, whether on one of the discs or between any pair. It now was crossing the entirely black one, indicating, as was the case, moonless nights.

On the level below, placed in a steel frame, were the gears that determined the progress of the wooden hand. Their proportions were those of a large clock, except for one (evidently in direct contact with the hand) whose extraordinary size signified a periodicity of abnormally great length. Although I could not measure this gear, its circumference was no doubt appropriate to the interval of a lunar month.

At one point on the rim of this gear, a short metal pin extruded laterally. Once in the course of each complete revolution, the pin would trip by its upward motion (the gear moved clockwise) a hook fixed to the topmost bar of the steel frame. The point of this hook was inserted in one of the recesses of a horizontal toothed rod, above which, barely visible behind the shield, was a slender spring. Spring and rod were joined at their right ends. Their position suggested that they followed the movement of the clock-hand in a horizontal line from left to right. Although the connection was hidden, the spring certainly controlled the clock-hand (a wire fitted vertically to the right end of the rod was possibly the means).

The purpose of the arrangement was clear. At the close of each lunar month, the pin on the gear's rim tripped the hook that held the rod in place, and the spring pulled the clock-hand (as well as the rod) from its rightmost to its leftmost position. It could then start anew its progress from left to right across the panel of moons.

A pendulum hung beneath the cage of gears. It had an ordinary shaft, but a singular construction had taken the place of the weight. A conical net of light wire, perhaps two feet high and as wide at the base, dangled at the shaft's end. Within it were a dozen silver herring which, all swimming in one direction, propelled the net with them, and with it the pendulum, which in turn imparted its movement to the mechanism of the moon-clock.

The pendulum was controlled in the following way. A cable made out of twisted wires of great fineness was attached to each side of the pendulum just above the joint of the net. Both cables then passed (one to the right, the other to the left) through a cluster of pulleys suspended from the steel frame above, midway between the top of the pendulum and the machine's outer edge. The cable, descending outwards from the pulleys, was fastened to an eye at the top of a pyramidal lead weight. Another similar cable, also tied to the weight, hung straight from the edge of the steel frame directly over it, where its tautness was steadied by a spring reel.

Underneath the two weights—one on each side of the machine—massive iron cups were fixed on sturdy rods half-buried in the sand. The cups were roofed with thin flexible metal.

The length of each cable was such that when the herring had propelled their net to one end of the pendulum's arc, the weight on that side would strike the cup beneath it. The diaphragm of thin metal would then emit considerable vibration into the surrounding water: this would sufficiently startle the fish to make them turn and swim away in the opposite direction. (By the time they recovered from their fright a new clash turned them round again.) The flexibility of the cup's surface also caused the dropped weight to bounce slightly, thus aiding the reversal of the pendulum's motion.

The tension of the reels, which exercised an upward pull on the weights; the ratio of the pulleys through which the cables passed; and the heaviness of the weights—all had been adjusted to a nice equilibrium that permitted the frail momentum of the fish to keep them, and the clock, in motion.

The herring were fed through a slender funnel-shaped net of threadlike close-meshed wire, connected to the pendulum net by an opening too small to permit the egress of the captive fish. The larger end of the feeding-net hung from a metal branch projecting from the rear of the steel frame. From the same branch was suspended a luminous smooth ball fashioned out of several tiger-cowrie shells—it floated in the mouth of the feeding-net as a lure to the small sea creatures that were the herring's food.

The entire life cycle of the herring took place within their prison; for how could the school have been replenished except by reproduction? There was no entrance for anything but animalcules. As for the dead fish, they drifted, eventually, through the bottom of the net. A fraction of an inch below the net's rim, attached by no visible means, floated a film of metallic dust. When a Cogito Swimmer probed it curiously with a fishing-spear, the point of his weapon disappeared. I recognized the presence of fleshmetal; and I did not doubt that the builder of the moon-clock had, like Inno Johnstone, used some sort of magnet (perhaps the wires of the net were magnetized) to hold it in place. The dead herring and any other waste matter would, in passing from the net, be volatilized by the suspended element, which also afforded invincible protection against attack from below.

On the sand under the net, the very color of sand, a fat ray lolled, alive but unmoving. Crabs of similar color rested on its back. They were perhaps waiting for scraps that might pass through the thin opening that separated the layer of fleshmetal from the net's edge.

The moon-clock stood on four iron columns sunk in the sand, one at each corner of the steel gearcase, under which the pendulum and its adjuncts hung, and upon which the panel of moons rested. The lower part was open to the water; but the gearcase was sealed with watertight glass panels, while an hermetic glass bell covered the clock face.

Surmounting the clock, at the very top of the glass bell, the builder had left a flat surface on which there were two figures, perhaps six inches high. One was a man, white, naked except for a crown of little faded leaves. The other was a black woman, also naked. The man was caught in a net of tangled white wire. Their features and limbs were carved crudely, except for the woman's vulva, which had been carefully represented as a mouth, with red tonguetip protruding between tiny sharp teeth. With one hand she lifted one of her breasts; with the other she held out a minute golden adze to the trapped king, who stretched his hands towards her.

On an exterior metal band that separated this scene from the panel of moons, two words had been roughly scratched: *Mundorys Lorsea.*

Having watched one of the Swimmers shoot the lethargic ray with a bolt from his undersea gun, I was unable to stand the cold any longer, and I swam quickly up to our boat. My companions took me back to the island at once. A hot drink at the hotel restored me.

The moon-clock having failed to yield the third answer, I decided to end my investigations. My long search had consumed more than the little money I had once possessed—I had even had to pawn the adze. There was nothing for me to do but return home and begin paying my debts.

APPENDIX I: DER MÜSSIGE SCHÖPFER

The following text is published with the kind permission of Mr. Walter Auerbach.

Gottlieb erzählte Marie seinen Traum von voriger Nacht.

"In einer grauen Stille schwebte ich nach oben durch den Himmel, an den Wolken und Sternen vorbei. Dann kam ich in eine andere Welt und dachte, 'Dies muss das Paradies sein.' Ich wandelte zuerst durch Auen, dann über bewaldete Hüge mit lieblichen Bächen, Dahinter lag die Stadt, ausgedehnt, aber überraschend still.

"Ich stieg von den Hügeln zur Stadt hinunter, aber just vor den ersten Aussenhöfen hielt mich ein erbärmlicher Anblick an. Ein Mann lag in dem Graben neben meinem Pfad. Noch niemals habe ich solch einen mageren Menschen gesehen. Man konnte durch seine Lumpen die Knochenenden sehen and wie sie am ganzen Körper beinahe durch die Haut stachen; und die Haut, grau and durchscheinend wie fettiges Pergament, fing in der Tat schon an vielen Stellen abzublättern und aufzubrechen an. Aus seiner Kehle kamen kurze Stösse eines keuchenden Stöhnens, die trotz Entsetzen and Ekel mir das Herz im Leibe umdrehten. Ich rannte weiter zur Stadt für jemanden mir zu helfen dieser armseligen Kreatur Beistand zu leisten. Kaum an den ersten Gebäuden angekommen stiess ich auf einen Polizisten, den ich aufforderte mir zu folgen. Bald waren wir bei dem Elenden. Doch als dieser sah wer bei mir war, stiess er einen Schrei des Schreckens aus und wurde dann so still, dass er mir nicht mehr zu atmen schien. Der Polizist jedoch, der zuerst gegen den Hingestreckten gleichgültig schien, trat nach dem Schrei auf ihn zu, erhob seinen Knüppel und versetzte ihm einen furchtbaren Schlag auf die Schläfe. Darauf salutierte er und machte sich auf seinen Weg in die Stadt zurück. Eine Zeit lang sass ich erschüttert and wie betäubt da. Schliesslich schaute ich den Betroffenen an und erschauderte beim Anblick seines Kopfes. Der Schlag hatte nämlich den Schädel eingedrückt und eine bläulichbraune Vertiefung von der Braue bis zum Scheitel gelassen. Doch als ich zuschaute, offneten sich die Augen und das keuchende Stöhnen fing wieder an, und zwar stärker als zuvor. Dann richteten sich die Augen auf mich, oder vielmehr nur eins von ihnen, denn das andere war durch den Schlag in seiner Höhle festgeklemmt worden. Das Auge blickte mich an, das Stöhnen hörte auf, und der geschlagene Mann verstummte vor mir grad so wie vorher vor dem Polizisten. Ich traute meinen eigenen Augen nicht und kehrte in die Stadt zurück.

"An der Stelle, wo ich den Polizisten getroffen hatte, stand nun ein anderer Mann, als ob er auf mich warte, und bald erkannte ich in ihm unseren Neffen Johannes, der gestorben war, als er auf die Universität zu Freiburg ging.

" 'Onkel Gottlieb!' rief er, als er mich erkannte. 'Herzlich Willkommen! Ich wusste nicht, dass Ihr es wart, doch hätt' ich's wissen müssen: wie stets ein Vorbild bürgerlicher Pflichterfüllung! Doch möchte ich Euch im Vertrauen sagen, fasst's nur nicht als Kritik auf, denn was Ihr getan habt, war ganz und gar richtig; ich möchte Euch aber sagen, dass man ihnen ausserhalb der Stadt ziemliche Freiheit gönnt. Es scheint, Ihr missbilligt, was ich sage, und ich muss eingestehen, dass sein Stöhnen fürchterlich war; aber was das nicht erst, nachdem Ihr den Engel gerufen hattet? Ich habe nämlich die ganze Sache mit angesehen, und mir schien, dass er sich ganz gut benahm, wenn man bedenkt, dass er sich ausserhalb der Stadt befand. Er war wirklich nicht zu laut und war im Graben wohl verborgen. Natürlich erschien er Euch unvermutet und versetzte Euch einen schönen Schreck. Doch Ihr solltet erst einmal die sehen, die weiter draussen sind, besonders die oben in den Bergen: einfach ekelhaft! Und wie die schreien! Im vorigen Monat musste ich dorthin gehen um etwas Haar zu holen. Es ist erstaunlich wie ihr Haar wächst auch in den widerwärtigsten Umständen. Für Tage konnte ich nichts als Zwieback und Milch zu mir nehmen. Wir müssen für die jetzige Regelung dankbar sein, obwohl es ihnen vielleicht etwas zu leicht gemacht und uns der Trost entzogen wird uns an ihrem Zustand erbauen zu können.'

" 'Sind das denn die Verdammten?' fragte ich.

" 'Wie drollig Eure Frage klingt, Onkel Gottlieb! Obwohl sie sich sicher wie die Verdammten vorkommen müssen,' lachte Johannes. 'Doch ist es besser, man lässt sie frei und offen auf dem Lande liegen und jammern als sie in der Stadt in die untersten Keller zu stecken und öffentlich zu prügeln. Man mag sie noch so gründlich knebeln und ihnen noch so viel Pein zufügen, die erforderliche städtische Ruhe wird nie erreicht. Sie sind nicht nur zu elend, sie sind einfach zu zahlreich. Stellt Euch vor: 190.000.000.000 bei der letzten Zählung. Ausserdem wurde der Platz, den sie eingenommen hatten, wieder frei und in sehr gemütliche Schlafsäle für die Handlanger umgewandelt; auf jeden Fall gemütlich genug für die. Doch sagt mir, Onkel Gottlieb: wie lange seid Ihr denn schon hier?'

" 'Ich war auf meinem ersten Wege in diese Stadt, als ich den Mann in Graben fand.'

" 'Dann seid Ihr ja eben erst angekommen! Du lieber Gott im Himmel, kommt hier 'rüber, wo man uns nicht sehen kann! Ach, Onkel Gottlieb, warum habt Ihr mir das nicht gleich gesagt? Gottseidank dass Ihr in Eurem Sonntagstaat seid; was für ein Glück! Ihr könnt Euch nicht vorstellen, wie empfindlich die hier in solchen Sachen sind. Früher, als der Andrang noch nicht so gross war, waren sie scheint's duldsamer in solchen Einzelheiten; aber heutzutage machen Kleider Leute. Ach, Onkel Gottlieb, ich freue mich ja so Euretwegen. Sie werden Euch sicherlich erhören and Ihr werdet ihnen von allem erzählen können: von Eurem Hof, Eurem Vieh, Euren Ersparnissen, die ihr so sorgfältig angehäuft habt. Jetzt könnt Ihr Euch zu all der Mühe gratulieren, Onkel Gottlieb, und Ihr werdet heil und sicher sein. Erwarten dürft Ihr nicht zu viel, Ihr werdet schon etwas schaffen müssen, wahrscheinlich auf den Lufthöfen, aber Ihr werdet so viele Tagelöhner haben, wie Ihr zur Hilfe braucht; und mit Euren Ersparnissen dürften sie Euch ein Leben zugestehen, dass Euch befriedigen wird. Es wird Euch auch möglich sein der Tante Marie den Weg zu ebnen; guter Einfluss schadet dabei nichts, obwohl Eurer natürlich nicht sehr gross ist. Aber das eilt alles nicht. Zuerst müsst Ihr in das Register eingetragen werden. Ich fürchte, es wird etwas lange nehmen, doch wisset, dass, wenn es einmal vorbei ist, seid Ihr für immer und für ewig untergebracht. Glaubt mir, das ist eine Erleichterung, wie Ihr sie noch nie erlebt habt, und wie Ihr sie nimmermehr erleben werdet.'

"Johannes nahm mich an der Hand und führte mich in die innere Stadt.

" 'Bitte denkt daran vorsichtig zu sein, wenn Ihr von Euren Besitztümern sprecht,' sagte er. 'Erwähnt nicht alles, zählt nicht jede Henne auf, Onkel Gottlieb, und vergesst dabei die Hauptsache nicht! Wisset, dass, obwohl es auf Geld allein nicht ankommt denn ein einflussreicher Beschützer kann einzelne Personen auch ohne einen Pfennig auslösen, es doch oft entscheidet, in welche Kategorie ein Ankömmling eingeordnet wird.'

" 'Sollte ich nicht lieber erst auf andere Verdienste hindeuten?' fragte ich. 'Die Liebe, mit der ich für meine Familie sorgte, die Mühe. . .'

" 'Ja, ja, Onkel Gottlieb, aber das wissen sie ja schon. Ausserdem macht sowas nicht viel aus. Es wird natürlich begrüsst und anerkannt, aber ist sehr schwierig zu bewerten. Dazu ist es auch noch so verbreitet, da gibt's kaum einen, der nicht eine Ausrede für sein Betragen fände. In dieser Hinsicht ist Güte hier die Regel und so allgemein, dass sie als Grundlage für die komplizierte Klassifizierung, die die Verwaltungsengel machen müssen, völlig unzureichend ist. Drum werden andere Gesichtspunkte beachtet, und einer davon ist Reichtum. Ihr müsst verstehen, Geld gibt's hier nicht, gerechter Himmel! Man wird mit allem nach seiner Klassifizierung versorgt. Ihr werdet gewiss mit Recht fragen, ob denn das rechtschaffene Leben eines armen Mannes nicht für mehr gilt als das eines Reichen. Doch im Grunde scheint es sich darum zu handeln, dass Geld den Reichen ein moralisch höheres Leben nicht nur erlauben sollte sondern in der Tat erlaubt. So offenbart sich, dass je ärmer man ist, um so weniger Zeit und Kraft hat man, um jene Wohltätigkeit auszuüben, welche den Wohlhabenden einfach eine Gewohnheit ist. In dieser Hinsicht ist es durchaus keine Ungerechtigkeit, wenn man das Geld bei der Anlage der Akten mit einbezieht. Man bemüht sich vielmehr Leuten das zu geben, was sie verdienen, und das bedeutet, wessen sie fähig sind, was wiederum von dem, was sie gewesen sind, abhängt. Sollte man einen halbverhungerten Wilden, der sein Leben wie ein Tier verbracht hat, genau so belohnen wie einen Mann, zum Beispiel einen Verwaltungsbeamten oder einen Dichter, der sich eines Dienstes höherer Ordnung fähig erwiesen hat? Das wäre wohl kaum gerecht.'

"Verwirrt klammerte ich mich an seinen Arm und wir gingen weiter. Wir wandelten durch manche saubere Strassen und als wir uns der Stadtmitte näherten, wurden die Strassen zu grossartigen Prunkalleen, welche mit Platanen bepflanzt und mit bunten, moosbewachsenen Ziegeln gepflastert waren.

" 'Sag' mir Johannes, lebt hier der liebe Gott?'

"Er deutete auf die prachtvolle Allee vor uns und erwiderte, "Könnt Ihr noch länger daran zweifeln?'

" 'Weiss er vom Mann im Graben?'

" 'Aber Onkel Gottlieb, um Himmels Willen! Der Arme hat schon genug durchgemacht; und er hat uns alles dies ermöglicht. Wäre es nicht zu undankbar, wenn wir ihm nicht wenigstens nun endlich Frieden sicherten? Er hat ihn uns beschert und noch weit mehr. Er muss seine Stunden nicht mehr länger mit der Obhut seines Reichs zubringen, sondern hat sich in seinen herrlichsten Palast mitten in seinem allerliebsten Park zurückgezogen, wo er von jenen betreut wird, die seine Wünsche am besten kennen. Seine Aufwarteengel bilden die höchste Ranggruppe im Himmel. Nur von Lobpreisungen und Anbetung umgeben, lebt er in Seligkeit; und seine Glückseligkeit ist unsere grösste Wonne. Vergebt mir meine Zähren, Onkel Gottlieb! Nun aber seht stolz und schneidig drein! Wir sind schon an der Registratur.'

"Wir waren en einem grauen Gebäude mit vielen Stockwerken angekommen, so gross wie eine Festung. Davor standen Leute in zwei Reihen; derer, die eintraten, und derer, die herauskamen. Als wir uns näherten, wurde die letztere von einer Gruppe aufgebrochen, die die grosse Treppe hinunterdrängte. Zwei uniformierte Männer hielten eine Frau zwischen sich und trieben sie zur Eile an. Ein purpur farbenes Krebsgeschwür bedeckte ihr Kinn. Sie verschwand mit ihren Wärtern in einer benachbarten Seitenstrasse, die ich vorher noch nicht bemerkt hatte. Manche solcher Gruppen verschwanden in dieser Strasse.

" 'Sie wird aus der Stadt entfernt,' bemerkte Johannes.

" 'Wie der Mann von heute Morgen?'

" 'Ja. Auch Krankheit wird in der Stadt nicht geduldet, wenn sie nicht vollkommen gutartig ist.'

" 'Aber die Ärzte hier sicherlich . . .'

" 'Ach, die Ärzte haben sich zur Ruhe gesetzt. Findet Ihr nicht, dass sie es verdient haben? In der Tat, nicht alle; da sind einige so vom Leiden besessen, dass sie ihre grossen Vorrechte aufgegeben haben, um mit den Kranken zu leben. Man hält sie für ein wenig verrückt. Könntet Ihr Euch vorstellen eine solche Entscheidung für alle Ewigkeit zu treffen?'

" 'Die Frau wird also nicht behandelt werden?'

" 'Wahrscheinlich nicht.'

" 'Aber wird's dann nicht schlimmer?'

" 'Wenn das der natürliche Verlauf ist, wird es schlimmer.'

" 'Dann wird aber doch die Krankheit sie eines Tages töten '

" 'O nein, was auch immer passiert, sterben wird sie nicht.'

"Wir waren an der obersten Stufe angekommen and waren beinahe im Gebäude, als mich auf einmal solch ein Grauen erfasste, dass ich laut aufschrie und vor Schrecken zitternd erwachte. Einmal wach, Marie, wurde mir auch klar, woher dieses Gefühl des Grauens gekommen war. Es war nicht der Schrecken über meine Vision, sondern der Gedanke, dass auch ich 'aus der Stadt entfernt' werden könnte. Und die Erleichterung, die folgte, war nicht nur die Erleichterung des Erwachens sondern das Wissen, dass ich auch dort drüben nichts zu befürchten hätte; und ich dankte Gott von tiefstem Herzen für all das Gut, dass er mir auf dieser Welt gegeben hat.

"Und jetzt erinnere ich mich auch; beim Aufwachen wandte ich mich Johannes zu; er lächelte, als er meinen Blicken entschwand; ich rief ihm nach: 'Dann ist's ja nur dasselbe?' und er erwiderte: 'Ja, Onkel Gottlieb, dasselbe, aber für immer, von nun an bis in Ewigkeit!'

"O Marie, Heil den Johnstones! Den verfluchten Johnstones! Den verschissenen Johnstones! Den Feinden des Bestehenden! Die haben sich behauptet und sind als Königen nach Alba heimgekehrt! Die Fut ihrer Zigeunerin sei mit argen Zähnen gespickt!"

•

APPENDIX II

A fragment in Mozart's hand may bear on the lost *Missa Fa Si Re*. The manuscript consists of thirteen measures for five unaccompanied voices, with the title "Kyrie" but no text. Listed by Köchel as an original composition, it was relegated by Einstein to the appendix of his revision of Köchel's work.

These are Einstein's notes on the fragment (Köchel, *Mozart-Verzeichnis*, Dritte Auflage, J. W. Edwards Verlag, Ann Arbor, Michigan, 1947, p. 832):

> Anh. 109^{vii} = 429^{a}. Anfang eines *Kyrie* für 4 Singstimmen von J. J. Froberger.—André, hds. Verz. F^{2}.

Abschrift Mozarts: Fitchwinder University, Swetham (Mass.), C. Washington Library. Das Autograph erst bei A. Johnstone, Baltimore, Kat. X (1776), Nr. 50, dann bei Syl. Doge,—London, Kat. 69 (Dez. 1911), Nr. 4211.

Anmerkung: Von Johann Jakob Froberger (1616–1667). Vgl. Denkm. der Tonkunst in Österreich, X, 2. Die Abschrift ist wahrscheinlich untergeschoben.

Literatur: G. Nottebohm, *Etwas über J. J. Froberger* in Mus. Wochenbl., Lpz. 1874.

The brevity of the editor's comments is in itself remarkable; but one is quite at a loss to explain the mistakes made by this punctilious scholar. There is no such Kyrie in the DTOe volume, and no mention of it in Nottebohm's article; nor is any mass by Froberger, extant or lost, known to musicologists.

As to the music, its style is certainly unlike either Froberger's or Mozart's, although it could conceivably be an exercise by one of them in the *stile antico*. It is to be noted that the soprano entrance is pitched uncommonly high, giving, together with the cross relation in the tenor, a singular emphasis to the alteration of the *fa-si ♭-re* motive to *fa si re*.

Lans-en-Vercors, December 1958–May 1960.

Des creux manoirs & pleins d'obſcurite

Dieu par le temps retire Verite.